I Might Be Bluffing
By Victor Robison
with Cliff Robison

Rock and Fire Press
Salinas, CA

I Might Be Bluffing

ISBN:
978-1-949005-20-2 (Print)
978-1-949005-21-9 (eBook)

Rock & Fire Press
Salinas, CA

N*I*A*C*IN denies any involvement.

Part I:
Trust Relationship Error

BENTLEY LAID DOWN THREE jacks, but they were no match for Yorga's straight. Chance shook his head and sipped from his beverage.

"I'm curious," he said, "Do you ever think you've set someone up? Not deliberately, of course."

"I sleep well, if that's what you're asking, Counselor," said Yorga. "I've honestly never tried to pin something on someone. And I've never taken a case to court if I didn't think we had the right guy." He stacked the chips and tossed an ante back into the pot. The others anted as well.

"I don't mean putting a frame on someone," said Chance. "I'm talking about an honest mistake." He shuffled the deck and dealt five cards around.

"Everybody makes mistakes," said Bentley. "That's why there's all those checks and balances. Folks like you, for example. If me and Yorga get a little too hasty, there's a defense attorney out there to rein us in." He laid down two cards and slid them towards Chance.

"Adversarial, not inquisitional," said Yorga. "I was talking to some French guys about how they do it, and the cops over there work for the judge. They tell you what to search, who to arrest, what to investigate. Then they make a decision who's right and who's wrong. I like it our way."

He laid down three cards.

Chance laid down one, and gathered all the discards into a stack. They all turned an eye to the fourth player, Lt. Jones, whose almost placid look was ruined by his twinkling eyes.

"I'm happy with these," said Jones.

Chance kept a straight face. Bentley looked like he'd been picked for decoy duty. Yorga was obviously thinking of throwing down his last two cards, but he held them.

"Suppose there was a case where the facts just didn't look right," said Chance. "Maybe it looked open and shut, but it was a little more complicated than that."

Chance dealt the draw cards; two for Bentley, three for Yorga, and one for himself. He made a face and threw down his hand into the discards.

"Inside straight never works out," said Jones. "But why don't you just say what you're thinking?" He pushed a couple of chips into the pot.

"A guy down at Soledad Prison wrote to me a while back," said Chance. "I couldn't take the case because of a conflict, but he had an interesting story to tell."

Bentley was frowning at his cards and tapping his stack of chips. Jones grinned at him.

"Don't let my draw fool you," said Jones. "I might be bluffing. It might be all smoke." Bentley shook his head anyway, and threw down his hand.

"You'll at least have jacks or better," said Yorga, "Or you wouldn't even try it. But I'll bite." He pushed in chips to match Jones. "So this story at Soledad, you allowed to tell us about it?"

"Well, the case is over, and you were already kind of involved, and he was never my client. Got a new trial, got acquitted, and walked away. So, while, on the one hand, I probably shouldn't say anything, strictly speaking, there's not much harm at this point."

"What happens at the table stays at the table," said Jones, pushing in a slightly larger stack.

"In that case, here's what he told me," said Chance.

The phone rang at about one AM. Normally, for me, that's one of two things: A client with a problem, or a client with a big problem. I wasn't asleep, but I was hoping to get that way pretty soon.

I caught it on the second ring, before caller-ID had a chance to tell me who it was. I probably should've let it ring a couple more times.

"Fermat Networks, Don here," I said.

"Don," said the voice on the other end, with a sigh of relief, and although it had been a while, I knew right away that it wasn't a client. It was Amanda.

There was a time that talking to Amanda in the middle of the night was no big deal. We were a thing for a while, and after we got over each other, we still stayed friends. Even late phone call friends. I'm a handy guy to know when things go wrong, especially computer things. But I don't restrict myself to electronics.

Back in the day, Amanda would call and tell me about men behaving badly. I'd let her ramble, and every so often we'd have a bite to eat somewhere. We'd take a break from that routine when one of us was involved, but otherwise, that was a fairly common thing.

Her record for a relationship was around 9 weeks, from just-met-him to had-to-dump-him. I got used to saying "uh-huh" while watching muted baseball games. Eventually we kind of faded out of that; it got longer and longer between those events. And then one night, out of the blue, she'd call again.

But that was then, say three or four years ago. So this had to be something big.

"Um, Don, listen, I've got a problem." Her voice shook a little. I had a feeling she wasn't calling because she was two eggs short for a cake recipe.

"What's wrong?"

"I've um, I, I." She came to a stop, obviously to get control of the growing vibrato in her voice. "Look, Don, can you just come over right now?"

"Right now? It's one in the morning."

"I need you. It's important."

"Should I call 911?"

"No!" She didn't quite shout it. "Um, no, no. Just come over quick, okay? Please?"

"Alright. You still on Palma?"

"Same apartments. 2A."

I was gonna make a joke about how 2A was not 2B, but she didn't sound like she was in the mood for a pun, so I let it go and told her I was on my way. I put on some shoes and headed across town.

The streets were quiet, so it was didn't take long.

That part of Palma Drive is next to Alisal Street. It's by that little corner shopping center with the pizza place, the bagel place, and the supermarket-turned-gym.

There was nothing obviously wrong from the outside; not like a biker gang in the courtyard or a zombie horde marching down the sidewalk. I parked my little Ford Ranger on the street and went up the front stairs.

The air was a little brisk, and I regretted not taking a minute to grab a jacket. I thought I might have a hoodie behind the seat of the truck; maybe I'd get it later.

It was a bit like Déjà vu trotting up the stairs outside her place. A lot of memories came back, some good and some less good. I wondered if I was making a big mistake, getting involved in an Amanda drama again.

I tapped gently on her door. She threw it open and gave me a big hug. Like I said, we hadn't even been telephone pals for the last three or four years, so that hug was a bit of a surprise to me. It felt good, don't get me wrong. Amanda knows how to hug.

Okay, so maybe she had a bad dream? Just needed a hug? Kind of a bummer to drive across town for it, but still, why not? I hugged back.

We stepped inside, with her still directly in front of me, walking backwards, staring into my face. She looked the same, with curly blonde hair, a nose that was just a little too big, and teeth that were just a little crooked. And cute as hell in spite of everything. She'd never be a supermodel, but if your friends saw you with her, they wouldn't ask why.

"Oh, Don, thank you, thank you! for coming over. I didn't know who to call. You've gotta believe me." She said it with a breathless intensity that conveyed urgency, as she gently closed the front door.

I rubbed her bicep. "I'm here for you, Amanda. What's going on?"

"About three weeks ago I met a guy."

At this point, I was hoping that I didn't drive across town in the middle of the night to hear a shaggy dog story about how Prince Charming had feet of clay. Still, it coulda been worse. You know, zombies or something.

"Right," I said.

"Well, I told him, 'no nighttime dates till we've had three lunch dates,' you know, the normal rules."

You might be catching on that there are a lot of people who do not know how to tell a story simply and succinctly, and Amanda is one of them. Honestly, for her, this story was moving briskly, but it still could take a while at that rate. I was probably going to hear about three or four of their dates, and a couple of phone calls.

"Yup," I said. I'd have sat down and made myself comfortable, but Amanda was still holding my elbows and staring me in the eye.

"I didn't know what he was like." She sniffled as she said it, and I was pretty sure that water works were on the way. I'd rather prevent that, when I can.

"It's not your fault," I said, anticipating the next part of the story. The sooner we could get to the crisis, the sooner I could get home to bed. "He's a jerk. You deserve better. He's going to regret this someday, but you will have moved on."

"What are you talking about?" she asked.

"You're telling me about this guy, right? You started dating, and now you found out that there's something wrong with him."

She started to giggle, not the funny kind, but the kind that she used to do when she was nervous, and something just too surreal for words. "Well, yes," she finally said. "There's, um, yeah, something wrong with him."

She turned me by my shoulders so that I was facing her kitchen, and I saw what was wrong with him. He was lying on the kitchen floor with a sword in his chest.

It was a Japanese sword, with a long, curved blade and a hand-woven handle. I'd seen longer ones, but this one looked like it had done the job.

It was sticking up from the left side of his chest, about where his pocket would be if he had shirt pockets. I'm no doctor, but that should have put it in his heart.

There was a pool of blood under him, but it wasn't growing. The edges of the pool seemed to be congealing.

"Did you call the police?" I asked.

She shook her head. "I was in shock, and now I've waited too long."

I stepped over, close to him, careful not to step in the pool of blood. It was probably pointless to check, with that much blood on the floor, but I did anyway. His jaw was open slightly. I pushed on his chin with my knuckle, and it moved, but not easily. He was cool to the touch. He'd been dead at least an hour or two. His chest wasn't moving. I couldn't hear any air movement in his nostrils.

A paramedic or a doctor couldn't have helped him. He was past the point of no return.

I looked up at her. "Tell me that you were having dinner with the Pope and the mayor, and that you just now got home and found him like this."

"No, Don," she breathed, her eyes wide open in terror. "I *killed* him."

It was just getting worse by the second. I should've let the machine take the call. But that's what they call hindsight. I sighed.

"Okay, tell me what happened."

She shook her head. "I was supposed to go out with him. We were gonna go dancing."

"And he didn't want you to lead? So you just stabbed him instead?"

"He *hit* me!" she whispered. Her eyes were wide, as if it were unthinkable. She seemed to be trying to stare the idea into my brain. "We, I, I, we were supposed to go dancing, and I said I wasn't feeling well." She pulled in her lips and just breathed rapidly through her nose for a moment. "He hit me, said he was going to … I, I grabbed the first thing… I thought he was going to kill me! "

I looked behind her, at bookshelf in the living room, where the sword used to have its own shelf. Now the brackets were empty. The saya, the ornate black wooden scabbard that had once held the sword, lay on the carpet, beside the bookcase.

She repeated her last phrase, nodding, crystallizing it: "He was going to kill me."

I tried to visualize the scene: He hits her, she steps back, grabs the handle, the saya falls off as she swings it... Except those things are kinda tight, aren't they?

"Was that sword important to you?" It was a silly question. It must have had meaning. It had its own shelf.

"My dad brought it back from Japan. It was a cheap souvenir, but it was from my dad."

Her dad, not her stepdad. Important distinction, at least in her family. She lost him when she was about fourteen, so the sword must have had significance. Well, sad as that was, the sword would be going away. To keep one of us from going away.

"Okay, look, you're safe now," I said. "We need to get this cleaned up. Got any bleach? Or peroxide?"

Having a task seemed to bring her back around to the practical world. I sent her to clean the sword while I dealt with the body itself.

She cleaned the blade and the saya with peroxide, in the bathtub, after stopping the drain. I used paper towels and bleach to reduce the horror in the kitchen, carefully loading them into a plastic trash bag. The trash bag went inside another bag.

Once the sword and its sheath were clean, she took a shower, and came out with her old clothes in a plastic garbage bag, even the trainers she's been wearing. The trainers looked expensive, but not as expensive as life in prison for murder.

By the time I turned and saw her in sweatpants and a tee-shirt, hair wet and draped over one shoulder, I had the body pretty much bleached up and wrapped in plastic garbage bags. Packing tape, the wide clear kind, held all the bags together.

All the loose blood was soaked up in rags, and splashed with bleach as well. The bleach breaks down the DNA, you know. So will peroxide.

With her help, I put him onto a carpet, which we rolled up and wrapped with duct tape. One body burrito, made to order.

It was almost three by then, and we managed to get all the trash bags down the front stairs without anyone turning on their lights or opening their doors to get a better look. The bags went into the back of my truck. The sword, now in the saya, went under the seat.

We took him out the kitchen door and down the back stairs. There is a kind of a porch that goes between the back doors of 2A and 2B, with steep concrete and steel stairs that go to a walkway right at the fence. It was a struggle getting him down the steps without dropping one end or the other, but we made it.

At one point I thought I was going to lose my grip, and Amanda looked like her hands were slipping. She started to giggle, and I had to shush her to bring her back to the present. Slowly, steadily, we got down the stairs.

No lights came on in the adjacent apartments, so I don't think anyone saw us. Or if they did, they ignored us and went back to sleep.

I know, you're thinking that we coulda just chucked him into a dumpster somewhere. Wrong. Even if there's not a camera on the dumpster, or somewhere nearby, and even if we found one that was unlocked, there's a camera on every garbage truck, recording what gets thrown out.

Honest. If you put stuff into your recycle bin, it had better be recyclable. And don't try to throw out hazmat like it's food waste. They'll get you.

Then we were out the side gate, across the street, and heaving him into the truck. It's a tiny truck, a Ranger, but he sort-of fit into the bed diagonally, with his head shoved under the toolbox on the passenger side, and his feet jammed into the rear corner on the driver's side.

I sat in the truck while Amanda ran back in to lock up and make sure that everything looked normal, or at least not like a crime scene.

As I was sitting there waiting, carefully keeping my feet off the brakes and trying to be invisible, I found myself wondering if I should've just called the police when I saw the body. She had an excuse: It would've been self-defense, especially after he hit her.

Except that she didn't have any bruises, or a split lip, or anything that would've corroborated her story. As far as I knew from just the evidence, she could've just gotten mad and run him through. Or she could have invited him over and stabbed him in cold blood.

Look, you help out your friends, right? But sometimes your friends just go too far, and there's nothing you can do for them. And if that were true, why was I helping Amanda hide a body?

What if she did it? What if this was cold-blooded murder? Even a crime of passion: It fit all the facts that I knew right then.

But, no, that was silly. This was Amanda we're talking about. She wasn't a murderer. She was always sweet and innocent, and her eyes made little inverted smiles when she laughed. She had that attitude of always being happy, no matter the situation.

I found myself wondering why we ever broke up. Maybe we cut off a good thing a little too soon.

And then I realized that I was helping her hide a body, so I stopped thinking of getting back with her. Something about killing somebody just moves a woman off of the dateable list.

A police car turned off of Alisal Street onto Palma. Of course, the one night that I'm sitting in a truck that has a dead body in the bed, the police decide to make a patrol. I started thinking up excuses, and came up empty.

I ducked down and kept my head in the corner of the cab, so there wouldn't be a shadow or a silhouette. The cop turned, not two car lengths away from me, into the parking lot of the former supermarket.

There were a couple of cars there. He scanned them with his spotlight, slowly prowled along the storefronts, then turned the spotlight off and exited onto Alisal again, headed towards downtown. I heard his transmission kick down a gear as he punched it.

I was watching the spot where his taillights had vanished, just past the pizza place, when there was a tapping on my window. I nearly jumped out of my skin.

It was Amanda.

"Have you got the sword?" she asked.

"It's under the seat."

"Cool." She ran around the truck and got in on the passenger side. When my heartbeat slowed back to normal, and I was satisfied that the police car wasn't coming back, we pulled away from the curb.

The body, carpet and all, went into an abandoned barracks over on the old Fort Ord. There are these big long barracks, from World War 2, and ever since the base closed in 1994, they've been slowing collapsing in onto themselves. They're covered in graffiti, filled with trash, and surrounded by bushes and weeds.

Anyone finding a body there would likely have no legitimate reason to be there, and would probably just leave it as it lay. Or that was my hope, at least.

We soaked it in rubbing alcohol, because we were out of bleach and peroxide by then. It might not completely break down all the stuff they can find with lab equipment, but between that and the body being semi-exposed in the old barracks, it should make it a lot harder to prove anything about where it had been.

Next we made a run out to Moss Landing beach, a secluded little place off highway one, a safe distance from the nearest houses. Despite a "No Fires!" sign, there were odds and ends from previous fires; small bits of wood that we supplemented with some driftwood and a couple of deadfall branches from the nearby stand of Eucalyptus.

We burned her clothes, at least the ones she had worn at the murder scene. For a moment it struck me just how incongruous it was: I was at a beach in the middle of night with a bonfire and a pretty woman. Except that we were burning evidence of a crime.

Eventually the last bits burned up, except for the parts that wouldn't burn, like zippers and buttons and whatnot. I dug a small pit down near the waterline, and buried the remains of the fire. In time, somebody with a metal detector might find those bits and pieces. If they did, more power to them. It wouldn't prove anything by then, and no one would still be asking about this guy.

The bags with the bloody and bleached paper towels and rags went into a couple of unlocked dumpsters out behind various restaurants in the greater Castroville area. Any remaining blood in them would be attributed to meat trimming. That done, we made our way back to Salinas.

She nodded off on the drive back, which was pretty reasonable, since it was pushing five AM by then. I took her to my house, and parked in the driveway.

She woke with a start, realized where we were, and gave me a look that asked just exactly what I thought we were doing.

"You get the couch," I said. "But our story is that you were here all night. Just keep it simple. Complicated stories fall apart. Simple stories are best."

"How did I get here?" she asked.

"You drove."

"My car is at my place."

"Okay, you called me, I picked you up, and here we are. But we've been here all night, since at least midnight."

She thought about it for a second.

"Why didn't we stay at my place?"

"In case I got an emergency call." As I said it, I glanced at my cell, just to make sure I didn't miss a client's emergency call.

"Why did I make you go and get me instead of just driving myself over?"

"You had a headache."

"Then I wouldn't be feeling up for staying over."

"You ran out of gas."

"Works for me," she said.

I got a couple hours of sleep, but not enough. I woke up to the smell of coffee and noises in the kitchen. To be honest, for a moment I thought someone had broken in. It was probably just because I was only half awake, but I honestly imagined that a burglar was having a cup of my coffee. Maybe the stuff I buy is really that good. People break in just to make a cup.

Then I remembered Amanda, and it all clicked.

I levered myself out of bed, made myself decent, and tottered into the kitchen. She gave me an odd look, like I should've straightened myself out a bit. I've been told before that I look slightly scary first thing in the morning.

"Hope I didn't wake you."

I growled something, and looked for my favorite coffee mug. I finally found it on the drain board next to the sink.

"I straightened up a little," she said. By straightened, she actually meant that she had reorganized according to her own plan. The kitchen hadn't been messy, but it also hadn't been set up her way. Now it was.

"Thanks for making coffee," I managed to say, pouring brain fuel into a mug.

"I couldn't sleep."

At first I thought that was an odd reason to make coffee, but then I realized that it had more to do with having something to do than with the coffee itself. I just shrugged and made a noise that I hoped was positive.

"We should get on with the next scene," she said. "We're gonna want witnesses." She pointed to the clock. Seven-thirty, right about time for people to be getting up to go to work.

When I was outside of my coffee, and had cleaned myself up a little, we got into the Ranger and I drove her home. I made sure to stop right in front of the courtyard to the apartments, in full sight of the people filtering out to the cars, on their way to start another workday.

I parked badly, with one tire on the curb. She jumped out, yelled a bad word, and slammed the door so hard I was afraid she'd break it.

I threw my door open and yelled, "HEY!" across the roof of the little pickup. She ignored me, marching purposefully towards her apartment. I chased after her

18

and spun her around by the elbow. Her eyes were burning coals, and if I didn't know it was all just an act, I'd have been afraid to say a word.

I shook my finger in her face and started speaking in a forceful undertone. "For score and seven years ago," I said, shaking my head, "Our forefathers brought forth upon this continent a new nation, conceived in liberty, and dedicated to the proposition that all men are created equal. We are now engaged in a great civil war—"

At that moment she made it a great uncivil war, by slapping me across the face. I hadn't known it till then, but she has got a talent for it. Olympic class talent, if that ever really becomes a thing. While I was recovering, she ran, sobbing, across the grass and up the stairs.

Several people were staring. I gave them all dirty looks and stalked back to my truck. All done, all through; one very memorable alibi was now neatly engraved in the minds of her cohabitants. Come a trial, they'd all recall her slapping me.

I got back home, and left the Ranger in the driveway. Despite the coffee, and despite being on call, I fell asleep on the couch. I woke up around noon, made some lunch, and went to dispose of the wakizashi under the seat of my truck. That's what you call those little swords, the ones that are shorter than the full katana.

The wakizashi was gone.

I looked under the seat again, and it still wasn't there. I shook my head, went back into the house, and had another cup of coffee. While I was doing that, I revisited all the things we had done: carrying the body down the back stairs, taking the plastic bags of clothes to my truck, and making sure that the carpet looked like a carpet, not a dead body.

I had a clear memory of shoving the saya, sword and all, under the seat of the truck.

There's a super-powerful flashlight that I keep in my toolbox. Even under its sun-like intensity, the sword was not there. I racked my brain, thinking about everything that we had taken out of the truck, but I had no clear memory of removing the wakizashi.

So I gave up.

I mean, suppose that it fell out while we were at the Moss Landing beach? Best case, some tourist thinks it's cool and takes it back with him to Nebraska. Worst case, the police find it. And so what? It doesn't link to me, or to her, or to the body, or to her apartment. It's just a souvenir sword.

Or suppose some kid broke into my truck and stole only that one item. Maybe while it was parked out front just now. Or maybe while I was getting my face slapped, though he'd have to be pretty bold. Again, there was no link back to me. No chain of custody.

Around then the phone rang, and I answered. It was a client downtown, and their PCs wouldn't let them log in. Ever since lunch – in other words, only a few minutes – they'd been staring at the screens, and they wanted me onsite an hour ago.

So I checked my hair, grabbed my briefcase, and headed downtown. It turned out the server software version had a glitch that makes the server forget the individual PCs. Then, because the server doesn't know the computer on the desk, it goes into Stranger-Danger mode and won't talk to it. We call that a trust relationship error.

Well, they had it bad. Over the course of their normal lunchtime, the server had developed selective amnesia concerning about ten PCs. It's a simple task to get them back into the server's good graces, and takes about five minutes each.

Then I ran an update on the server, so it wouldn't happen again, and set the server to reboot about an hour after they all wrapped up for the day.

Through the miracle of modern software automation, I emailed the invoice to their accountants before I even left the premises. A nice little bit of business to offset the unproductive morning. I would've still been okay, even without it, because the monthly contract service fees are my bread and butter.

I had two or three more business-related calls, one of them billable, and then Amanda called me.

"Amanda," I hissed. "What are you doing?"

"I know," she said, "But his car's here. If they tow it, there'll be a record that he was here."

She was right. I read a lot of murder mysteries, so I know that what gets people arrested is that they forget a little detail somewhere. And then some clever cop – or if they live in a tiny English village, some clever amateur sleuth, usually the town vicar – figures out the tiny little thing that the crook overlooked. And it looks like what I overlooked was a car.

"What does it look like?"

"It's blue."

"Lots of cars are blue."

"It's one of those boxy Scandinavian ones. With the seatbelt commercials."

That gave me a clue. I thought I knew what kind she was talking about, and they're not overly common in that neighborhood.

I waited until what they call nautical twilight, where there's a little bit of light still in the sky but it's not easy to see things well. When I was a kid, we would've said that the streetlights were just about to turn on.

I parked about a block away. There was a boxy little blue car by her apartments, alright, but it wasn't the one from the seatbelt commercials. It was a Tarq Firefly.

They're kind of rare in the US, but that doesn't mean expensive. No offense if you're Estonian, but these things are made in Tallinn, and the quality control is a little weak. I'm not sure that the doors are supposed to lock. The doors on this one didn't.

They did make a tell-tale squeak and a pop when I opened the driver's door. The ignition switch was broken and turned without the key. So far, so good.

The problem came when I looked out the windshield. There was a lot more dirt and grime on the car than should've accumulated in less than twenty-four hours. But maybe he'd been driving it like that. Or maybe he didn't drive much at all, and had practically been living at Amanda's place. None of my business.

The windshield wipers just pushed the dirt into shiny streaks. The washer was a single very anemic stream. I could have spat more water, with more pressure. The water didn't actually remove any dirt, but did turn it into a fine gray mud.

I finally wound up getting an old burger wrapper from my truck and using it to wipe away enough mud that I had a porthole to look through.

The next chore was finding a place to dump it. I didn't want to be pulled over driving it, so I stuck to residential streets. I crossed West Alisal Street, turned down University, and followed it to Central. That took me to the college, and into the college parking lot.

I didn't bother getting a slip from the machine, but I did take a moment to wipe the car down for fingerprints before I hurried off into the night. I took a shorter route going back, but I still tried to avoid anywhere that there might be a camera. It was almost eight, maybe nine, when I got back to Amanda's and recovered my car.

The thing you won't know about a Tarq Firefly – I certainly didn't – is that they have a certain unique feature that makes them very attractive for terrorists. I don't know the details, but there have been around four or five car-bombing in the Western region of Europe lately, and all have been Fireflies.

The next morning's news featured a possible bomb scare at Hartnell college: A car of a type known to be used by terrorists had been left by a shadowy figure shown on the parking structure's security video. Fortunately for me, the video was distant and grainy, and only showed my back, in only a few frames.

I watched the news until there was another update: The car was not a bomb, and had been towed away, but police were searching for the car's owner, an elderly man who lived on Palma street.

You heard me. An elderly man. Not, for example, the guy in the body burrito that we dumped out at the old Fort Ord. I got the wrong boxy blue Baltic car.

That night, I made another twilight raid. There was a blue Volvo in the parking lot, near the Bagel place. The dust on the windshield was more consistent with a one-day stay than the Firefly had been.

I carefully examined every other car in that lot, and near those apartments. Nothing else fit the description. Most of them were made in Detroit or Yokohama. There was one that was made in Spring Hill, and there were two from Munich.

My next stop was a car parts dealer on South Main. Volvos aren't as easy to break into, but they're still not tough. I got two door cylinders, one ignition cylinder, and a couple of specialized tools.

Funny thing: You need door and ignition locks for a Volvo, you have to go to the Volvo dealer, and they cost a fortune. Also, they take three weeks to get. But the old AMC Pacers, if you remember those; they had the same door and ignition cylinders. Identical.

So you go into a parts store and ask for Pacer cylinders. Nobody still has that car, but guaranteed, the parts place has got 'em in stock. And for about a quarter of the Volvo dealer price.

Anyway, I changed the lock cylinders, all three. Yes, it was overkill, but that way if a cop pulled alongside me, I was driving a car using a key that actually worked for that car. Not like the Firefly, where it didn't need a key at all.

Nothing suspicious. Nothing at all to make a cop look twice. Much safer that way.

I couldn't use the college again. They apparently have cameras, plus the police would now expect other stolen cars to show up there. They might have had it staked out.

I picked Dayton Street, over in the industrial area, off Abbott Street and Harkins Road. I parked it in a big parking lot, between two huge warehouses. Now, if it was found, not only did it not give away where it came from, it also didn't work with any keys that might be found on the body. If the body was ever found, you know.

I thought about what to do with the keys.

Keeping them would be stupid. Having any kind of link to them would be a bad idea. Best to lose them where they wouldn't be found. I can't tell you why, but it seemed like a good idea to throw them onto a warehouse roof.

It took me four or five tries to lob them that high, and the outside security lights had come on by then. I was finally rewarded by the metallic sound of keys landing on a sheet metal roof.

It was a much longer walk back to Amanda's place, but I kept telling myself that if it kept me out of jail, it was worth every step.

"I see you and call," said Yorga, pushing in chips to match Jones.

"Full house, kings over queens," said Jones.

"Not good enough," said Yorga, laying down four jacks. "Caught two of those on the change."

"Two great hands in a row," observed Chance. "Anything up your sleeves?"

"Just lucky," said Yorga. "Sometimes you get the cards, and sometimes the cards get you."

Chance passed the deck to Jones, who shuffled three times and then dealt five cards around.

"So tell us about Fermat," said Bentley.

Yorga grunted, and Chance took that as a cue to continue his story.

So there we are, hoping that the bulldozers get to that one particular set of old barracks before someone finds the body. I mean, if it turns up in the debris, after things have been mixed around, who's gonna be able to tell what happened to him, or how he got there, right?

Any clues will be hopelessly mixed up with random stuff from a collapsing old building.

Yeah, no such luck. About three weeks after the blue car shuffle, someone jogging with a dog reports that a barracks smells like decomp, and next thing you know, the body is on the news. Lead story at six.

My phone rang at six-ten. Caller ID says it's Amanda. She hangs up before I can answer.

I call back and get her answering machine. "Yes," I say, without giving a name. "I saw it too. Just stay cool. It's gonna be fine."

A couple hours later, she does it again. I call back again, and get the machine. "Amanda!" I hiss into the phone. "You're gonna get us caught. Knock it off."

A couple hours later, again. The message I leave this time is a bit sharper. "Amanda. You're making me mad. Stop this. And answer your phone next time."

That's it for a while. Then about a week later, maybe two, she called me again, and when I picked up the phone, she was still on the line.

"Amanda, we need to talk," I tell her.

"I thought there was nothing to talk about."

"Well, that's it. You need to stop calling me."

"Don, you ever think about us? About the old days, about how it was?"

I wasn't gonna say it, but sometimes I did still think about the old days with her. Sometimes I still do. It was nice sometimes. She could be really sweet when she wanted to be. And she could be jealous and controlling when she wanted to be.

"You know," I said, "That was then. This is now. It's water under the bridge, the moving finger writes, all that."

"Which finger, Don? This finger?"

I knew, even without seeing her, which finger she was holding up.

"Amanda, come on. Look, it didn't work out before, and it won't work out now."

She said a bad word.

"Amanda, behave yourself," I said. "We're not out of the woods here. There's still a few bad things that could happen here."

She hung up. A few weeks passed, and I forgot all about it. Until the day that I couldn't.

In the Salinas Police station, there is at least one tiny triangular interview room. It's rare to see a triangular room, and I have to think that there's some reason why it's triangular. If so, it's too deep for me.

The long wall is covered with something like painted canvas over fiberglass, with tiny holes in rows and columns. It's like some kind of soundproofing. There's a very small table and two small metal chairs.

I sat in one chair, and a guy in a suit sat in the other chair. He wasn't looking at me. He had a laptop, and he was wearing headphones. As nearly as I could figure, he was listening to music videos.

There was a larger man in the room as well, and he *was* looking at me. I was in the chair farthest from the door, and he stood directly between me and the door. He was very close to the door, but in that room, it's tough not to stand next to the door. If they wanted to rearrange the furniture, all they needed to do was to turn the doorknob.

"I'm Detective Sergeant Yorga," he said. "This is Detective Bentley." He gestured to the guy sitting in the other chair.

I nodded, but the other guy never looked up.

"So, Mr. Fermat, any idea why you're here?"

"Um," I shrugged. "No clue, actually." Well, aside from the fact that I helped to cover up a murder, but we left the body and all the clues in a different jurisdiction, so no, I have no reason to be here. Nothing to be afraid of at all. That didn't stop me from feeling my pulse in my chest.

"We were wondering if you could clear something up for us," he said. "Just something that we don't quite understand, you know."

I shrugged as casually as I could. "Sure."

"There was a kind of an odd thing that happened a few weeks ago on Palma Drive. Do you know anything about a blue Tarq Firefly?"

"Um, no," I said, trying to knit my eyebrows. "Was there a traffic accident or something?"

"Or something," said Yorga. He nudged Bentley, who clicked a couple of things and then spun the laptop around to where I could see it. There was a badly focused photo of a street scene, from somewhere above the street. It might have been from a window, maybe a window of the apartments behind Amanda's place. Maybe a security camera. Did either building have cameras?

There was a blue car, and a shadowy figure standing by the driver's door. Yorga tapped a button and another photo replaced the first. The figure was getting into the car. Another photo, and the car was driving away.

"You know anything about this car or this guy?" asked Yorga.

In the TV shows, this is where people "lawyer up." The problem is that calling a lawyer, just because a policeman showed me an out of focus photo of someone getting into a car – well, that would be like admitting, off the record, that it was me.

"Doesn't ring a bell," I said.

"Somebody told us you were in this neighborhood about this time. We thought you might have seen somebody stealing this car."

I tried to give him a blank look. Bentley spun the laptop back around.

"Funny thing," said Yorga. "They didn't do anything with the car. People steal cars because they want the car, maybe. But not this guy. Left it by the college."

Bentley took off the headphones, draping them around his neck. "Sometimes," said Bentley, "People steal a car for parts. Or they want an untraceable car to use for a crime. But this guy dropped the car off at the college in just about the time it takes to drive there." He spun the laptop around again, and a camera from a high angle showed the car pulling into the parking structure.

"They don't have a camera that shows the guy getting out," said Yorga. "Too bad on that, huh? We'd have the guy for GTA."

Bentley looked me in the eye. "But why d'ya figure the guy stole the car and drove it straight to the garage?"

I shrugged again. "Joyride? I'm not a cop, so I don't know why people do stuff like this."

"Yeah," said Yorga, nodding. Bentley spun the laptop back towards himself. "Joyride. Perfect. Except, you know what? People who take joyrides like to break things. They drive really fast, drive through rose bushes, spin donuts on someone's lawn, crash into poles so they can make the airbags go off."

"This guy," said Bentley. "It's like he just wanted to get across town or something."

"You know what?" asked Yorga. "Maybe he just didn't want that car parked on his street."

"He coulda called the abatement people," said Bentley. "Abandoned cars, they take them away, right? No need to break into it. No need to commit a felony."

"Yeah, I dunno," said Yorga. He took the top of the laptop and spun it back towards me. "Now, you see this guy here?"

Yes, and I recognized him. It was me, getting out of a blue Volvo on Dayton Street. It was far away, and from a very high angle. One of the warehouses must have had security cameras.

"You think he looks like that other guy? The first car thief?" asked Bentley.

"There's something we should tell you, Mr. Fermat. You don't have to say anything to us." Yorga was staring intently at my face.

"You have some rights," said Bentley. "You have the right to remain silent, and anything you say can and will be used against you in court. You have the right to have an attorney present during questioning. If you desire an attorney and cannot afford one, one will be appointed for you without charge."

"So," said Yorga. "Do you understand your rights?"

"Yes, I believe so," I said. I tried to sound puzzled. "Am I being charged with something?"

"We just have a few more questions," said Yorga. "We'll get this cleared up and you can go back home. We just need you to help us out here."

"So you do or don't think this looks like that other guy?" said Bentley.

"Well, it's kind of high up," I said. "A bad angle. Can't really tell how tall that guy is – nothing to compare against for height, you know."

"True," said Yorga. "That's what our own people said about this photo. You've got an eye for this, Mr. Fermat."

"What's kind of curious – or it makes me curious," said Bentley, "Is that two blue cars are stolen, both are moved way across town, and there's no real damage to either one."

"Just the ignition cylinders," said Yorga. "And you know what the guy did on this one? He changed the locks. Changed the ignition and both door locks. Brand new cylinders, all three."

I tried to look surprised, even amused.

"We checked the Volvo dealer," said Bentley, conspiratorially. "Didn't sell any locks. Dead end there."

"Yeah, but watch this," said Yorga. He tapped a key, and the figure by the Volvo moved. Now his arm was raised and there was something shiny in the air.

"Looks like he threw something," I said. I wasn't giving anything up by saying it. It was pretty obvious that the shiny thing had been thrown.

"That's what our people said," replied Yorga. "So we went on the roof and found these." He dropped a clear plastic bag on the table. It had red tape across the top and contained a set of car keys.

"Brand new keys. And they fit that Volvo. Imagine that. Changes the cylinders and throws away the keys." Bentley shook his head in disbelief. "That makes me think that there's a guy who really doesn't want any blue cars around."

Yorga turned the laptop back towards Bentley.

They were toying with me. They knew everything. This was the time to throw Amanda to the wolves. *Save yourself,* said the little voice in my head. I drew in my lips and looked up at Detective Yorga.

"So we just tried to guess where he came from," continued Yorga. "Checked other reports of possible car thefts. We found out – and you'll never believe this – that blue Volvo started off less than a hundred feet from where the blue Tarq was stolen. What do you think about that, Mr. Fermat?"

"Closer to fifty feet," said Bentley.

Bentley turned the laptop again. This time, the camera was somewhere inside a storefront, and it was a jerky, grainy video. Through the front window, in the dusky dark, a man could be seen tugging on a tool while standing beside a blue Volvo. The license plate was clear, but the face was obscured by the store's "Closed" sign.

"This time, you kind of get an idea of height. He's yanking out the little clip so he can get that door cylinder out." Yorga glanced at the photo and glanced at me. "About your height, eh, Don?"

I shrugged.

"Kinda looks like you, just you know, superficially, right, Don?" He gave me a look. "Anything you want to say about this?"

I shrugged and tried to look innocent.

"So, the real question is this," said Bentley. "Why would someone want to get blue cars away from Palma Drive? Boxy blue European cars?"

"Maybe," said Yorga, "It was because some kind of a crime happened on Palma Drive."

"Funny thing," said Bentley. "That blue Volvo? The one that the car thief paid extra attention to? Left in an industrial area, changed the cylinders? And just threw away the keys?"

I nodded.

"We found out that it belonged to the guy who was found dead on the old Fort Ord grounds. That body the jogger found. You heard about that?"

"Just what I saw on the news."

"Yeah, sad case," said Yorga. "And someone just rolled him up in a carpet and dumped him. Probably figured nobody'd look before the building got torn down, right, Don?"

"Well, if you say so," I said. "I couldn't guess."

"So what was the guy's car doing by Palma Drive? And why did someone want it to be anywhere except Palma Drive?"

"See," said Bentley, "We figure that the first car was a mistake. Guy mixed up his boxy blue cars. Anything you want to say about that? Anything at all?"

"It's an interesting story but I don't see…"

"What it has to do with you?" said Bentley. "Oh, we're coming to that."

"We figure it was a crime of passion," said Yorga.

"Car theft is a crime of passion?"

They both laughed. "No," said Yorga. "The murder. That was the crime of passion."

"Wouldn't that be Marina PD, or the sheriffs? Or maybe the Feds, since it happened on the old base?"

"Since the murder probably happened in Salinas," said Yorga, "We took jurisdiction."

"You think the murder happened in Salinas? You think it was murder?"

"You got those two questions in the wrong order," said Bentley. "You should have done it like this." He opened his eyes like dinner plates. "Murder? You think it was murder? Here in Salinas?" he relaxed his face. "See, that's how you play that scene. The other way, you're burying the punch line."

"Like Robert Preston," said Yorga. "Right here in River City."

"I'm not acting," I said. Yorga gave Bentley a grin and a look, and the look said, *Can you believe this guy?*

"Rhymes with pool, right? Here's what I think happened," said Bentley. "There's a girl. There's a guy.

There's another guy. Somehow it works out that both guys and the girl are all in the same apartment at the same time. Bad situation.

"One of the guys has no right to be there, you understand. So the other guy pulls a wall-hanger of a sword and stabs him. Then he tells the girl to keep her mouth shut or else, and they hide the evidence."

"That does explain the thing with stealing Baltic cars," said Yorga.

"Yeah, what's GTA next to a murder charge?" replied Bentley. They could have been talking about a football game, if it weren't for the quick glances at my face, for my reaction. "What do you think, Don?"

"I think it's a nice story," I said. "But don't start fitting me for that frame."

Bentley turned the laptop back towards himself and tapped a couple keys. He pulled out the headphone plug, and I heard my own voice on Amanda's machine.

"Yes, I saw it too. Just stay calm. It'll be fine," I said, on the recording.

"You probably had just seen the announcement that we identified the body, right?" asked Yorga. He didn't wait for an answer. The next recording was also my voice.

"Amanda, we need to talk."

There were several other calls, from the day she wouldn't answer the phone. They were spliced together, not in the order I said them. In this context, they sounded like I was hounding her; warning her to stay quiet. Where had they gotten those tapes?

There was a tap at the door, and Yorga stepped out for a moment. When he stepped back in, he was smiling. He gave Bentley a thumbs-up sign.

They spun the laptop around again, and I saw Amanda, sitting in this very room. Or maybe another room, just like it. Yorga tapped a key.

"He *attacked* me. I thought he was going to kill me," she breathed, just the way she had told it to me when she called me to help with the body.

"He was going to *kill* me," she gasped. It had that same note of breathless eyes-wide incredulity that I had heard that night. Yorga stopped the video.

"We searched your house," said Yorga. "We got a warrant while you were sitting here with us." He handed me the folded blue paper. "We found a short decorative sword, made in a Japanese style. If it were real, I think they'd call it a waka-wa-..."

"Wakizashi," supplied Bentley.

"Yeah, what he said. And it's exactly what our informant told us to watch for. And it's consistent with Mr. Nash's wounds."

Yes, I wondered, *but how did it get from under my seat to somewhere in my house? I never took it out of the truck.* Then the word *informant* seeped through to my brain.

"Better still," said Bentley, glancing at his phone for a text message, "It has a bloody thumbprint. That ties a person to the body and to the murder weapon. Suspect plus body plus weapon, that's a conviction in a bag."

A tiny voice in the back of my head named someone who had access to my truck, and my thumb, and the blood, and my house. I told that little voice to shut up.

"We really don't need you to say anything at this point," said Yorga. "But if you were inclined to try to clear this whole thing up for us, now would be the time."

"Okay," I said. "Look, I helped her cover it up. But it was self-defense. Just like she said. You heard her. He was trying to kill her. You heard her, just now."

Yorga looked at Bentley, then back at me. They were both smiling. He tapped the key again, and I heard Amanda's breathless voice, confiding in the camera.

"I thought Don was going to kill me. He said if I didn't help him, he'd do what he did to Clark. I thought – I thought he was going to *kill* me."

"That's *his* story," said Bentley. "I don't believe any part of it. We had a solid case there: The thumbprint, the murder weapon, the crime scene, the witness. We had motive, jealousy; opportunity, he still had a key to her place; and means – That sword was right out in the open, he admitted it. It was a good bust."

He laid down one card. Yorga threw in all five, and Chance kept two. Jones kept three, and then dealt the replacements.

For a few minutes, there was no sound except the rattling of chips.

"I told you right then not to get mixed up with her," said Yorga, with a shrug. He didn't like the new cards any better than the first hand, and tossed them towards Bentley.

"It was her idea," said Bentley. "I told her that I don't date crime victims. She said she wasn't a victim; she was a survivor."

"Unindicted co-conspirator, more like," said Yorga. "What happened to her?"

"She ran off to Vermont," said Bentley, pushing in a couple of chips. "That's where she was from. Look, the jury already handed down the verdict before she even asked me out."

"Well," said Chance, "You did him a favor. You dating her gave reasonable grounds for a new trial. His lawyer told the judge that maybe you were seeing her from day one." He matched Bentley's small wager. "Planning a check-raise there? Small bet to get us in, then raise it on the second round?"

"How'd the *de novo* go?" asked Jones, matching the other two.

"Acquittal. All the evidence was stale, and two key witnesses were tainted. I think he moved to San Diego."

"See," said Bentley, "It's all checks and balances." He slid three large stacks of chips into the pot. "Are you in? Keep in mind, I might be bluffing."

Part II:
The Reckoning

YORGA COUGHED INTO HIS hand. "Since I'm sitting this one out, I guess it's my turn for a tall tale."

"I'm shocked you would accuse me of prevarication," said Chance.

"Anything for an edge, right, Counselor?" said Jones, as he matched the others' chips.

"You might recall a Lieutenant named Licowicz," posed Yorga. "Big guy with a taste for beer."

"Before my time," said Jones. "Though I heard a one-sided story about him and a Mobius strip club."

"We passed in the doorway," said Bentley. "I got here about two weeks before he left."

"I remember a bit of skullduggery over on Lincoln Street," said Chance. "Not sure I recall any details. Or, none I can speak about."

"So, I worked with him maybe two months. Not directly. I hadn't taken the sergeant's exam, and Sergeant Sanchez mostly ran the day-to-day in homicide."

Bentley laid down a king-high flush. Chance and Jones threw down their cards, as Bentley raked in the chips. "I remember that nobody wanted to talk about him," said Bentley. "Almost like it was officially hush-hush or something. But that was a long time ago."

"Well, we went down to the bowling alley one night, and after a few beers, he told me a story. Might actually have been a couple days after his retirement party. But I had a beer, and he had several, and he told me a story that he swore was true. Take it or leave it: It's what he told me, and it went like this:

I hate Merlot. Not the wine. Well, I don't like wine either. I'm more of a whiskey kind of a guy, or if you don't have whiskey, beer will do fine. Simple tastes for a simple mind.

I admit it. I'm not a smart guy. Not like Merlot. Merlot's some kind of genius, some Einstein or something. I guess I can't complain about that, since it's how a big dumb cop like me made Lieutenant. Still, I hate that guy.

Maybe hate's a strong word. Geez. What do I know?

Here's the thing: Some case comes in and nobody's got nothing on it. I give Merlot, near as we can figure, the time and place. He comes back to me with a photo of the guy who did it. Just like that. Sometimes he even gives me a video.

What the hell, right?

But here's the thing: He always tells me, "This isn't evidence. You can't take this to court, 'cause you can't prove where you got it." Only he says it nicer.

I told him I'd subpoena his butt into a witness chair or die trying. He says it wouldn't matter. He can't prove that he took the picture, so the case would get thrown out. I say, hey, the picture proves you took the picture. He says to ask an ADA about that. You know, a lawyer.

And besides, if I ever screw him over, he stops helping me. I know a good thing when I see it. I'm not gonna goose the duck with the golden eggs, you know?

Anyway, who's the schmuck that has to compare 200,000 mugshots, and tell the brass I got a hunch that it's this guy here, and then go shake the suspect till he gives it up? Well, until I made Lieutenant, it was me. Now, I tell the Sergeant that we got an anonymous tip that it was this guy here, or that the murder weapon's in a tree by the park, and the sergeant sends somebody else to check out my hunch, or to make waves till somebody floats to the top and confesses.

Captain thinks I've got a bunch of snitches out there, or C.I.s, we call 'em, sweeping the streets for dirt. He wonders if I'm a little dirty, and if I'm playing both sides. I always tell him I'm not smart enough for any of that. He knows it's true.

Anyway, I was down at that little pub on Gabilan Street. The one that used to be English and then turned into a sports bar. Yeah, went from trivia nights and stout beer to football and American lager. TVs everywhere. You know the one.

Merlot come in with a woman. That, I expected. Problem is, I knew this woman. She used to be married to a meth cook out in Prunedale. And way back in high school, I used to date her sister.

"Evening, Glennis," I said, before he had a chance to introduce us. "How's tricks?" She knew what I meant.

She started to smart off, but he stopped her. "Hey, Babe," he said, "Go get me one of those drinks, huh? You know." He nodded towards the bartender. She shot me a look, but she went.

"What corner is she workin' these days?" I asked.

"Be nice," he said. "I told her I'm meeting the money behind one of my screenplays."

"Good luck getting money out of me," I said. Then I remembered why I was really meeting him, and slipped him a pair of hundreds under the table. He looked down at it and raised an eyebrow. Okay, I'm thinking, but this better be good. I slipped him another pair of centuries. That's out of my pocket, you know. Having a CI is one thing, but gettin' the department to pay for 'em is another.

"Yeah, so here's one for a murder case that hasn't come up yet," he said, putting an envelope on the table. "But I might not be available when it does."

I put down my beer. "If you know about a body, you better report it," I said. "I let you slide on a lot of crap, but murder – that's not gonna fly."

"Nobody's dead yet," he said. "But just in case, keep this handy." Glennis came back with the drinks, so I put away the envelope, downed the last of my beer, and went on home.

Three AM, my phone rings. That's never good. I'm hoping it's a wrong number. I'll spare you the details, but it's about Merlot. He's still at the bar. 'Cause somebody stabbed him in the eye.

I got to Glennis' place around ten AM. I figured she ought to be up by then. You can see her house from Blackie Road. It's on the hill, facing towards Orchard, so from the highway you can see the backside of the house and part of the yard. Her house is the old blue one with the big scorch mark on the back. Two of the windows are boarded over, and the third has a coat of soot. I guess she never bothered to clean it off.

Her most recent ex had a little accident. Closer up, you can see where the shed used to be in her back yard.

It's just a bare patch with some little furrows spreading out from the center. Like a little crater, kind of.

I think I said she was married to a meth cook. That didn't work out so well. Nothing grows right there. Must be from all the bad chemicals.

I went around the front — you can't pull off the highway onto that part of Blackie any more. Too many accidents. So you gotta weave around the roads where you can get off. Anyway, it's a house that looks like you'd expect for a meth dealer. Small, single-story, got windows with aluminum frames. You turn a crank and they open out. Real cheap stuff.

Paint on stucco, ugly pale blue. Flat roof, top edge of the roof, the paint's peeling off. Yard full of weeds and some bushes. One of them has those blue leaves that look like an octopus. Ugly as hell. Cortes, in traffic, he says they make tequila from those things.

I go up to the front door — It's a door for inside a house, and the top layer, the veneer, it's all cracked and blistered as bad as the cheap paint on top of it. There's a nail sticking out about head high. Tiny little nail, like somebody put up a wreath once. If she and Merlot were, you know, friendly, well, she might need that nail.

She must've seen me coming, 'cause she yanked the door open before I even knocked. "What the hell!" she yelled. It was like, you know, *You got some nerve, showing up out here.*

I let it go. "Look," I said, "What time did you last see Chris?"

"Chris? Who's Chris?"

"You didn't even know his name? Merlot, first name Christopher. You were at a bar with him last night. Ringing a bell?"

"Oh." She shrugged. "Wine man. Right. Yeah. I'm gonna be in his movie."

"Is that so?" I said. Merlot must've been pushing this movie thing pretty hard. Far as I know, he's never sold a script in his life. But if that's the line he was selling, sure, why not. And, oh, yeah, I'm the money. I almost laughed.

"You don't think I could be in a movie?"

"You prolly could," I said, just to keep from starting a fight. Fact is, she took better care of herself, she might be okay. She's a little too thin for my taste, not super skinny, but she doesn't have much of a butt or nothing like that. Some curves maybe, just not exactly sculpted like a supermodel.

A bit of makeup, maybe do her hair, she might be okay. But no way in hell I'm gonna say that to her.

"So how's Betsy?" I said.

"That why you're sniffing around?" she asked. She grinned and kinda shook her head, like *look at this dork, looking for Betsy.* "She moved to Arizona, had a bunch of kids. Fat as a house now. You out chasing chubby women these days?"

"I'm just being social," I said. "Plus we need to talk about this wine guy."

"People call him that cause he's named Merlot," she said, only she called him Mur-Lot. I may be a big dumb cop, but I know you say it Mur-Low.

"I know," I said. "Look, here's the thing: When did you leave the bar last night?"

"Right after you left. He said he needed to see somebody about a bill. I finished my drink and I left."

"How'd you get home?"

"I drove."

"You drove him to the pub?"

"No, we met at my work. He said we could walk to the bar, it was right there, so we did."

"Where you workin' these days?" I was thinking, *What street corner?* but I kept a straight face.

"Mid-town market, on Central and Lincoln. What's it to you?"

"You a cashier?"

"Yeah. You got a problem with that?"

"No," I said. "I got no problems at all. Fact is, I'm doing real good. But you said you left right after me. What time is that?"

"I got home, I guess … well, the news was on. The Monterey station, so ten-something. Why? What baloney are you trying to frame me for?"

"Nothing. Geez. It's about Merlot."

"What did he do? I need to go bail him out of jail or something?"

"No, you can't bail him out. This Bill guy that he was gonna go see…"

"Not Bill, you idiot. A bill, like a tab. Like settling up. Like a debt."

"Okay, so who was he gonna see?" Geez, like pulling teeth. Come to think of it, her sister was the same way, back in the day.

"How the hell would I know? If he told me he was going to see you, I never woulda gone. You done stinkin' up my porch?"

"He's dead," I said. I don't just blurt stuff like that, but she was getting on my nerves.

She didn't say nothing. She just looked at me. Her eyes were narrow, like she thought I was trying to pull something.

"Somebody stabbed him in the eye, and I need to know who he was gonna see."

"You're full of it," she said.

"Fine. Suit yourself. Can I use your bathroom?" I didn't really need to go, but sometimes you can look around a little on your way to the john. A meth bust might make her more talkative.

"Hell, no," she said, and slammed the door in my face. The whole front of the house shook, and the cheap windows rattled in their frames. Well, that wasn't very helpful at all.

By the time I got back to the station, I coulda used a beer. Better still, a boilermaker. But I try not to do that when the sun's up. Personal rule. You drink too heavy in the daytime, bad stuff happens. Next thing you know... Well, let's not go there.

Captain's yelling when I walk in. "There he is, the man of the hour," he shouts. Everybody looks at me, then they turn back to what they were doing. Nobody wants a piece of what's gonna happen.

What the hell now, right?

In his office, I close the door.

"I've got you all figured out," he says. "You and your solve rate. I know how you do it."

For a second I almost say that's over, what with Merlot goin' belly up, and then for another second I wonder how the hell he knew about Merlot. But then I realize he doesn't know diddly.

"Sergeant Sanchez. She's going over to major case. Let's see how the hell you survive in Homicide without taking credit for what Sanchez turns up."

"She tell you that?"

"Do I look stupid? I figured it out by myself, which is something I don't think you can do." He grinned like one of those crocodiles from the nature programs. "Let's see how you do without your right arm."

48

Sanchez wasn't my right arm, she was my left arm. Merlot was my right arm. But I didn't say nothing.

"I've been asking myself for years now, how does a bonehead traffic cop get a gold shield, much less make lieutenant – and then one day it dawns on me. Sanchez. You've been stealing her glory."

No, I'm thinking, *the way a bonehead traffic cop with a 92 IQ gets a gold shield and bars on his collar is by busting his hump studying for exams, and tracking down leads from miracle pictures.* But I'm not gonna say that, either. Yeah, 92, you wanna make something out of it?

"You got nothing to say?"

"Aside from me saying that you just stink? Nothing at all, Captain."

"Watch your mouth, Licowicz." He stared at me for a second, then he smiled again. "I'm looking forward to watching that miracle 90% solve rate drop to 0%. And that's when I can go the union and tell 'em you lost your edge, and I should fire you for cause."

"What if you're wrong about Sanchez?" I said. "What if it's my able leadership that's making her look good?"

"You really think that's the case?"

"No, she's smart. She gets things done. Not afraid to work. But somebody has to say which cases, how to work 'em, and who to look for. And that's where I come in."

"You got a crystal ball or something?"

For a second, I almost said that, no, they're like everybody else, then I got what he meant. And I did have a crystal ball, or at least somebody who could read 'em. But he was dead.

That evening, I was down one boilermaker and a beer when Glennis came walking into the bowling alley. She wasn't too sober, neither. Her feet were coming down a little too far apart, and her legs were sort of circling a little bit with each step. Like they were made out a rubber or something.

Prolly not meth. Vikes, maybe. They make you kinda loopy. Earlier, I was gonna try to bust her so I could get something about Chris out of her. But right then, I didn't give a rat.

"You bastard," she said.

"Back atcha," I said. Chris, he woulda said something clever, made everybody laugh. Except me, I never got his jokes.

"You killed him, you bastard." She said it like she was reading the weather report off the TV. Her lips even moved, just like when she reads.

"Dint kill no one," I said, annoyed. I looked back at the ballgame on the big screen. The way they got it set up, there's a score screen for this alley, one for that alley, then a TV. So on all the way down the room.

That's why I was there, by the way. Beer and baseball.

"You bastard," she said. "You killed him and now you can watch TV like nothing happened."

"Whadda you been smokin', Glennis?"

"Why? You gonna bust me and then stick me with a shiv, like you did with Merlot?"

I almost said I wouldn't stick her with the bartender's shiv, but that woulda kept it going. I ignored her and stared at the TV.

"So what the hell were you doin' there?"

"Doin' where?" I said, without takin' my eye off the game. They got a stand-up double, no outs, and the guy at the plate is showing a bunt. You kidding me? You ever see a bunt play that works? Ever?

"At the bar. You were there to see Merlot."

I looked up, and she was standing at my table, hands on her hips. "None of your business," I said.

"He told me you were the money. That's a laugh. You drink all your money. That's why Betsy left you."

"Get outta my face," I said, and turned back to the ball game.

She backhanded me, right hand, all the power she had in those scrawny little arms. I exploded outta my chair and shoved her away. Her heel caught another chair and she went down on her butt.

"Stay the hell away from me," I said. "Or next time they'll carry you out."

She got up on her feet and staggered her loopy self out through the snack bar and into the street. I took a look around in case Galahad was ridin' by, but most people in a bowling alley know not to get between a man and a woman who are fighting.

Good way to get your butt kicked, is what that is.

Top of the ninth, my team's down by two and two out. One on base. Three and two count. Next pitch is a foul tip. Talk about your sudden death, right? And that's when the uniforms come in. Out of the corner of my eye, they lean across the counter of the snack bar, talk to someone, and then they start headin' towards me.

Another foul tip. Catcher jumps up and rips his mask off, but it's in the stands behind home plate.

"Evening, Lieutenant," says the tall uni with the two chevrons.

I hold up a finger as the joker at home plate swings at smoke. Ending the game on a K, that's just sad. I turn to the kid with the chevrons and raise one eyebrow.

"Heard there was a domestic in here earlier. You see anything, Lieutenant?" He knew I was an Ell-Tee, even in my street clothes.

"I just saw my team get robbed, but the ballpark's out of your beat," I said. "Aside from that…"

"You got a red mark on your face, Lieutenant," said the other guy. I looked at him. Rookie, fresh haircut, and his shirt was ironed with those little creases up the pockets. He turned red when I looked at him.

"Nice to see you fellows," I said. "Now, near as I can tell, nothing in here needs your attention. So why don't we call it a night?" I stood up, picking up my jacket off of my chair.

"Can we give you a lift, Lieutenant?" asked the kid with the chevron on his sleeve.

"I got this," I said, and walked out the door, the same way Glennis went. I didn't watch 'em, but I knew what I woulda done. I'd have hung back for a minute, then headed for my squad car and called in an all clear on the possible 415 at the bowling alley. No uni is gonna make trouble for an Ell-Tee.

But maybe these guys were connected to the rat squad. Or maybe the Captain put 'em on me. So I took a stroll down Main Street and left my car where it was. I know what you're thinking, okay, but look, I had one beer the whole game. Well, two, counting the boilermaker. But I was okay. I'd been in the bowling alley more than an hour, and that's one beer off right there, plus it takes more than one beer to put me over. I'm a big guy.

So the fresh air is getting a bit chilly, and I'm thinking I ought to go back and get my car anyway. Cold air, a walk down the street, that's prolly burned off enough alcohol to make me legal, right?

But something tells me that's a bad idea, and I walk on down to Pine, head a couple blocks east to California, and let myself into my apartment. And then, just as I'm unlocking the door, I remember the envelope.

I paid Merlot four hundred dollars for an envelope, just in case somebody got killed. And guess what, Merlot got himself killed. So I started looking for the envelope, and I laid down on the bed to rest for a moment.

Suddenly the sun's up and the radio's going and I'm wearing clothes that look like I slept in 'em.

A shower doesn't help much. What was in those beers? Or maybe it was the whiskey I had with 'em. Forgot to mention that.

I get a fresh suit, do what I can with my hair and my face, and I'm trottin' down the stairs two at a time. And just as I got to the parking area, I realized that my car's about a mile or so away, behind the bowling alley.

An old lady walkin' her dog gave me a shocked look. Musta been somethin' I said.

But look, it's still early, right? I'm running behind, a bit fuzzy around the edges, but it's not eight yet, plenty of time for a twenty minute stroll. I'll tell the Captain I stopped for a donut.

He'll ask if I stopped for a beer as well, that's what he thinks of me, but I'm gonna shrug that off. Gotta play nice for a while.

My car's a twelve-year-old Celica, and as soon as I seen it, I said another bad word. The doors were open. I had some papers in the seats, you know, a newspaper and some burger bags and a couple of coffee cups. I keep long hours and a messy car, you got a problem with that?

But anyway, some joker must've rifled through my car. Prolly looking for somethin' he could sell. Good luck with that, you know?

When I get over to it, it's okay. They didn't bust the ignition or nothing like that. The glove box is open but the registration's still there. None of the windows are broke, but this is one of those cars you can open pretty easy with a coat hanger.

These days, harder to find a coat hanger than to open the door, you know?

I clean up the parking lot – not that I'm expecting a littering citation, but then again, I don't want to get warned off by the bowling alley people. I like watching baseball there, where I can get some peace and quiet. The only thing better would be to get a big screen of my own, and drink beer at home.

But that's how you go alcoholic.

I don't bother calling it in. Nothing's missing, or nothing important enough for me to notice. Plus it looks bad. Makes the uniforms laugh at you behind your back.

I got to the station probably eight-thirty, loosely speaking. As I got to my desk, I looked over at the Captain's office. He's got a glass door, and his office is right across from mine. He gives me a dirty look, then he points to his left shirt cuff, like maybe I don't know what time it is.

I nod and raise my eyebrows, kind of shrug, like *You know how it is, Captain.* And then I went over the reports. Captain forwarded one over to me, reported domestic dispute in a bowling alley. Unknown female had departed the scene. Uniforms made contact, saw nothing, dropped it. But they told the Captain they saw me, obviously. Why else would he send it to me?

Domestic? Hell, there's no way I'm getting domestic with Glennis. Surprised me the uniforms bothered to put it in their logs. But I'm glad they did, because it tells me they don't have my back. Not like the old days, and the thin blue line, right?

Some other stuff that's routine, don't park in the handicapped spot, charity drive's coming around again, stuff like that.

Then there's one report that catches my eye. It wasn't for me; it was one of those that goes out in case you can match it up to something you see later. Witness reported seeing a woman abducted by two unknown men, at a bar off of Monterey Street. Argument, altercation, nobody saw the car, no faces. And I got a feeling in the pit of my stomach.

See, here's what I'm thinking: Somebody wanted something from Merlot, and stabbed him trying to get it. And someone saw me meet him – Hell, they might have already been there when I paid him for that envelope. That's why my car got raided. So what if they also followed Glennis, and what if she staggered all the way to Monterey Street before they had a chance to grab her?

I looked out my door towards the Captain, but he's chatting with some suits. Probably getting the menu for the Big Hat BBQ. Rodeo's next month, you know.

I pulled out my personal cell phone – I carry two, one for the job and the other for not the job. We're not supposed to do that; Rat squad says it makes us look like we got secrets.

I called Glennis. Yeah, I had her number. I've got about a million numbers. I know a lot of people, and most of them are people I don't like. Goes straight to voicemail. I hang up and call back. Straight to voicemail. I send her a text, like *Call me wen u get this* or something like that. No response. Crud.

Then Sanchez sticks her head in the door and tells me that there's a DB – that's a dead body – out by the industrial park on Harkins. And I got another funny feeling in the pit of my stomach. The first thought I had was to run out there with them and to see if it was her. But that's gonna make questions, like *Why was the Ell-Tee the first guy on the scene?*

So I need to dawdle for a bit. The place where they called in that abduction was about four blocks from the police station. It's closing in on nine. Should be somebody there, maybe. Cleaning people, maybe, if it's the kind of bar that bothers with that.

I walked to the bar, but it was locked up tight. I walked back to the station and got in my car. Then I thought about the envelope Merlot gave me. I didn't remember ever taking it out of the pocket of my coat, so I drove home and looked for that suit. It was in the bag for the dry-cleaner. Lucky thing I didn't send that bag in.

When I got back to the car, it was ten easily, pushing toward quarter after. Now, if I go to the murder scene, it doesn't look like I've got a personal reason to be there. It looks like I'm supervising my people, following up on activity, keeping abreast of the situation. All that stuff the Captain is always yelling about.

All the stuff I'm gonna have to actually do to keep a decent close rate, now that my ace in the hole in gone. Which made me think I should check to see if the guys that went through my car took anything out of the trunk. Nothing important in there, but I keep gloves, crime scene tape, odds and ends that are helpful when you're investigating.

I popped open the trunk, stared for a second, and then I slammed it shut again. All of a sudden, I didn't wonder where Glennis was. She was in my trunk, staring up at me with her good eye. In the bad eye, she was wearing an ice pick.

It's been a long time since I had a blackout, where I was drunk enough that I either passed out somewhere or I had a hole in my memory. I could put together everything I did from the time I saw Glennis at the bowling alley till I got into bed. So I was pretty sure that I didn't do it.

And then I realized that the ice pick cinched it; she was killed by the same person who killed Merlot. I don't even own an ice pick. But she was in my trunk, which points to the guys who broke into my car. And that means I'm stupid as hell.

Okay, look at it: I fought with her at the bowling alley. It was her fault, and she left on her two feet, but I left maybe half an hour later. Close enough people might say that I followed her out. And I didn't report the break-in, so I can't prove somebody broke into my car. Like I said, all the windows are fine, nothing really missing, no evidence of the crime, right?

And she's in my trunk. Put it together, what does it spell? It spells me going to prison. And that's not a good place for a cop.

So I've got two choices. I can open my trunk and turn myself in, which is the same as shooting myself in the head, or I can play it close to my chest, which means getting the body out of my trunk. It wasn't really a choice, if you think about it. I was committed the second I slammed the trunk.

For the fifth time in as many hours, I wished Merlot were still alive. For one thing, his genius brain would've come up with a good idea for what to do with Glennis. Aside from putting her in his movie, that is.

Him and his movie scripts. I dunno if they were even any good. I never bothered to read any of it. Dunno if he was serious, or just using it as a line with the ladies. Not that it matters now, you know? He's not gonna be getting no prizes for best movie.

The only idea I had for what to do with Glennis was to take her home. There's really not a good place to dump a body where you can't be sure someone won't see you. Especially not during the daytime. Trust me, I know, I'm a detective.

First thing, I've got to drop by the homicide in the industrial park. I drove out there just as Sanchez was peeling the latex gloves off of her hands. I parked across the street from her car and jogged over to her.

"What you got?"

"Break-in at a garage. Looks like the guy didn't want to pay for repairs, so he tried to get his car before it was ready. Went under the car to check things out, jack let go, and that's that."

"Open and shut. That's how I like 'em."

"Coroner called it misadventure." She looked around, bit her lip, and then looked me in the eye. "Guess the Captain talked to you already?"

"About you moving to Major Case?"

"Yeah. I didn't ask for it."

"Hey, I got no problem with people moving up. You gotta do what's best for you. I'll miss you, but I'll make it work. This is a good move for you."

"Captain says I could probably make Ell-Tee on the next exams."

"Prolly could. You're smart, and you work hard. I hope Major Case works out good for you, seriously. No hard feelings."

I looked around.

"Listen, Sanchez, I got a couple of errands. Need to follow a couple of leads on the Merlot case. If somebody asks, I'm looking into a witness."

She nodded, still not real sure if I was serious about no hard feelings.

Glennis' place, I told you about it earlier. It's back from the road, so I got my car up by the house pretty easy, and the bushes hid me pretty well, except for those creepy octopus-looking things. I looked around, made sure I couldn't see the freeway.

I put her in her bedroom, on the floor, and I tried to put her as close as possible to the way she was laying in my trunk. One of the ways we know if someone moved a body is if it's in a different position from the way the blood settled.

Speaking of blood, there wasn't any. There was hardly any in my trunk, either. What was in my trunk, I cleaned out with some cleanser I found under her sink. But the coroner was gonna know right away she didn't die where I put her.

Second best, I found some bleach by her washing machine and splashed it around next to her body. Once it dried up and soaked in, it would look like someone cleaned up the blood.

Okay, so what was gonna put me here, when we came back to investigate? Fingerprints, maybe? Okay, I was here a couple days ago, interviewed Glennis about Merlot, notes are in my notebook. Maybe I used her john, took a second to snoop, looking for something about Merlot. Who's gonna say I didn't?

It's always the girlfriend or the boyfriend that done it, right? Most of the time, that's who we look at first. So it makes sense that we'd check her out. I came back today, knocked on the front door, got no response. I went away. End of story.

Later, week or so, maybe more, I'd come back, get a bad smell, worry about her, and call for back-up. The longer it was before the body was found, the better I could sleep at night because there would be less chance of it looking like I brought her here.

I left, as careful as I could.

OK, yeah, before you get excited, I checked and made sure she was dead. For one thing, she was cold, for another, she was stuck in one position. Plus, the ice pick. If you saw it, you wouldn't ask no questions. So, no, calling it in wouldn't have helped nobody.

There's an advantage to being a little slow, and that is, you tend to forget stuff. Like I managed to forget I moved a DB in my trunk and left it in Prunedale. The first couple of nights, it took three beers and a couple of shots to forget that real good, so I could sleep. But I did it.

Well, that brings me to Friday the thirteenth. Sanchez was packing out of her desk in homicide, and moving her stuff over to a desk in major case. We had a lady killed her husband for cheating on her. She was sitting there smoking a cigarette when the uniforms arrested her, and she admitted it straight up. So that counts for a win on our scorecard.

The guy that the car fell on, the day I found Glennis in the trunk, that one was ruled a misadventure, which is big words for doing something he shouldn't have done, and it bit him in the butt. So that one didn't count either way. It was just something that happened.

Typical murder rate in Salinas is about 20 per 100,000, which makes 30-40 in a year. I dunno why they gotta say that it's per 100,000. The population goes up and down by time of year, about 150,000 to about 200,000. You do the math, 'cause I don't like math. They should just say, we get about 30 to 40 murders a year.

So far this year – and they got a way they like to say that, too – we closed 13 out of 15. One that's open is Merlot, the other is some guy got shot in Closter Park, and nobody knows nothing. It's like this guy was sitting there minding his own business, and oh, what's this, I got a hole in my shirt. Well, look at that, there's a bullet in me. I guess I'm dead.

It's like that sometimes. Nobody hears anything, nobody sees anything, nobody knows the guy. We found out who he was, and we found out what kind of bullet killed him – 9 mm, from a pistol. And that's all we got. Nobody wanted him dead, except whoever shot him.

Normally, I'd give that to Merlot and work back from whatever picture he gave me, but when we found this guy, we couldn't pin down when it happened. Merlot said to call him when we found out, and then I forgot about it because we had other stuff going on. Now I'm looking at it again. I got nothing else.

Wait... There was that envelope Merlot gave me. You'd think I wouldn't forget an envelope that I paid $400 for. So in the privacy of my office, I get out that envelope. It's still sealed. I rip the end off and slide the papers out. There's two papers.

First one, it's a nice color picture of somebody's hand, holding an icepick. I can see from about an inch above the wrist, the whole fist, back of the hand, and parts of the handle above and below. The point is sticking out of the fist on the thumb side. There's some stuff in the background, a little bit out of focus. I couldn't tell which way to hold the picture, 'cause there wasn't anything that was up or down, one way or another.

I look closer, and there's an old tattoo, the kind you see on old sailors or on people that did time. The lines aren't real straight and they've spread out, like somebody did it with a felt-tip marker. Except it's faded, kinda faint brown, and real ink doesn't do that, so he was in jail when he got it. Probably made of pencil lead and soy sauce or something.

It's got lines that cross each other, and there's an X on two corners, and another in the center square. Like somebody was playing tic-tac-toe and forgot about O. Solitaire tic-tac-toe. Maybe that's a thing.

So I looked at the second picture, and that one made me go pale. I closed my eyes, opened 'em again, and stared at it. It was me, and I was in Glennis' house, putting her body on the floor.

Okay, so what the hell? What do I do with a picture of me committing a crime? And how the hell did Merlot get it before I even done it?

My mind was racing. Was there a camera in Glennis' place? Even if there was, when Merlot gave me the picture, Glennis was still breathing. So did he fake the picture? If he did, how the hell would he know it was gonna happen?

What I really needed right then was a beer.

I seen the Captain's door open up, so I real smoothly turned that picture over, put a folder on top of it, and when he walked in, I was staring at the other one.

"What's that?" he asked, like I'm maybe reading a letter or something. Pretty rude, you ask me.

"Maybe a clue in the Merlot case," I said, casual as I could. I held it where he could see it. He snatched it out of my hand.

"Awfully bad picture, you try to take this with the lens cap on?"

"I didn't take it. Think maybe it came off somebody's cell phone. Informant gave it to me, wouldn't say where he got it."

"What's that tattoo?"

"Somebody's bad at tic-tac-toe," I said.

He gave me a look, like *don't try to be smart with me,* and he threw the picture back on my desk. "You ask gangs about it?"

"I just got this today," I said. "First chance I've had to look at it was right now."

He grabbed the envelope off the desk. Good thing I didn't stick that other picture back in there. "Fingerprints on this?"

"Prolly just my informant. Come on, Captain, let me do my work here."

"Where are you on that Closter Park thing?"

Look, he knew as well as me that the Closter Park thing was dead as a hammer in a milk bucket. Prolly the guy was ganged up, somebody else didn't like his colors. Bang. Happens sometimes. But he had to throw that in my face, just to bust my chops.

"Lookin' into it," I said.

"Look harder," he said. "And approve these expense reports before you go home." He dropped a folder on my desk and walked outta the office.

Expense reports. If anything ever makes me go off the deep end, it's gonna be expense reports. I hate numbers. But I can't just fake 'em, because then somebody'll slip something in there that bites my butt. I gotta look at each one, is it legit, does it add up, did they put on the receipts, all that stuff.

Then I gotta compare it to my budget. Whoever thought up budgets didn't like me much, you know? More numbers.

Anyway, I forgot about that picture of me, and mostly forgot the picture with the hand. Around six, I got the expense reports done, and I took 'em to the Captain's office. I woulda dropped 'em on his desk, same way he done me, but he's gone.

Forget him. I shoved the folder under his door. He's got a inbox, same as everybody, but I figure he can trip over 'em when he comes in. Teach him a lesson.

Then I thought about the tattoo picture, and I went and got it to show to Sanchez. Except Sanchez don't work for me no more, and she's gone for the day anyway. Just not my day. I stuck it in my coat pocket and walked to my car.

So I'm thinkin' about my trunk. I mean, Glennis was in there that whole night, and whoever done it is prolly thinkin' I don't know yet. Prolly waitin' till the stink makes somebody open the trunk, and then I got some explainin' to do. Anyway, maybe she left some of that DNA in there.

I don't know anything about DNA except what I see on TV, but those lab guys, they can look at a carpet spot and tell that it was from this guy or that guy or whoever. Anyway, I gotta make sure they can't do that. So I got a plan.

That midtown market where Glennis was workin', they got a help-wanted sign out front. I walked in and bought a forty. For you pansies that only drink wine or whatever, that's a great big bottle of beer. Forty ounces, you get it?

Guy at the counter looked at me funny, because I guess guys in suits don't normally buy a forty. Well, if I had my way, I wouldn't be in a suit. But anyway, that forty gets spilled in my trunk. Ooops. Kinda sloshed it around a little bit.

When it was dry, I got some old socks and underwear that's too small for me, and threw that stuff in my trunk. One thing I know that stops somebody searching for stuff, that's another man's skivvies. Even though they're clean. Somebody opens my trunk, they're not sticking their hand in to search for nothing. Some kind of phobia people got.

So now I gotta wait for the other shoe to drop. Somebody makes a trap, they gotta spring the trap. Me, I gotta just be casual and keep calm and wait.

Sundaram, in Gang Task Force, he usually has some suds over at the Brass Rail before he goes home. Sure enough, he was in there. I took a barstool next to him.

"Hey, 'Deep," I said. Everybody calls him 'Deep, short for Sandeep, which is the short part of his first name. He's one of those guys, when the form asks for his full name, there ain't enough room on the page.

He nodded, kind of *Hi, but don't bother me right now.* Kept sippin' his suds.

"Meant to talk to you at the office," I said, ignoring the look he gave me. *Yeah, I know it's after five*, I'm thinkin', *but gimme a chance here, okay?*

"I'll be back in Monday," he said. "Nine to five."

"I'm in a hurry on this," I said, "I just got one question." I pulled the picture out of my coat pocket. "You ever seen a tat like that one?"

He glanced at it, real casual, then he set his beer down and picked up the paper. "Where'd you get this?" he asked.

"Informant," I mumbled. "You know that one?"

"Prison tat," he said, but I already figured that. "It's a code, kinda like Mason's code. There was a group using it, kind of an Illuminati thing, secret society stuff, but they collapsed years ago. That pattern, that's the letter 'N.' "

"Think that's from this guy's name?"

"Nope," he said, putting down the paper. "Probably from the name of the group. Their name started with N. Find me Monday and I'll look it up for you."

"So this guy was prolly in a prison gang that starts with an N."

"They weren't really a prison gang," he said. "I heard about them in Anti-terrorism, when I was on LAPD." He finished his beer and put the mug on the bar. "Homeland Security had them on the watch list for a while, then they collapsed. Dunno why they'd get bad tattoos."

He got up and left, maybe because he was a one-beer guy, or maybe because he didn't like my company. I can understand that. Sometimes I don't like my company. Me, I stayed and had a couple. Dunno how many. Then I walked home.

I got up early the next day and walked downtown to get my car back. Lot number 8, that's the one across from City Hall, and where I park when I got a chance. Mostly full during the day. So as I'm rounding the corner by the old firehouse on Salinas Street, low and take hold. There's a black-and-white cross ways behind my car. The officer, he's walking around it, shining his light in the windows, stuff like that.

He sees me and nods to me. "Morning, Loo-tenant." I nodded back to him and walked up to the car.

"Whatcha got here?" I asked.

"Someone called it in, possible abandoned car, trunk smells like decomp. Waiting for the CSU before we pop the trunk."

"You try running the plates?" I asked.

He blushed a little. I'm not in charge of patrol, so I really can't bust his chops too much, but still, rank has its privileges.

"Just about to," he said. He got back in his car and starting talking to the radio. He's tapping on the laptop that's mounted to his dashboard, too. After a few minutes he jumps back out.

"Registered to an Elton Earl Licowicz," he said. Then he looked at me again. "Any relation?"

"I might have an interest in that car," I said. "Fact is, I might be able to open the trunk for you." I pulled out my keyring.

"That's your car, Lieutenant?" he asked. Just about then, the CSU truck pulled in. Then another black and white, to watch the fireworks.

"DMV don't lie," I said. "An' like it or not, Elton Earl is what my mama named me." I held out the keys. "Go ahead, pop that trunk open."

Now, I'm not exactly looking forward to a bunch a uniforms poking in the skivvies in my trunk, even if they are clean. It ain't dignified. Still, beats them finding a body, and handin' 'em the keys shows I got nothing to hide. Of course, that doesn't stop me from wondering if some SOB put Glennis back in my trunk.

So the sergeant that was in the second black-and-white, he comes over to me, and the uni I was chatting with gives him a rundown on what's going on. Like the owner of the car walkin' up, and me being in charge of homicide, and an Ell-Tee. I gotta hand it to the Sarge, he was a cool customer. Doesn't take even a minute to think, just turns to me, casual as ordering a beer.

"Lieutenant Licowicz, is this your car?"

I nod and grin.

"Would you mind, just for the moment, you understand, would you mind handing me your off-duty piece?"

I raise an eyebrow. He's going by the book, so he's on solid ground. He could get pushy if he had to. But he doesn't.

"Just for our safety, you know, the regs and all," he said. But his right hand is touching the bottom of his pistol holster, pulling it out slightly. That puts the hammer against his side and makes it nearly impossible for someone to draw his gun.

Now most people who aren't cops don't know it, but that's also a position where we practice drawing our guns at the range. I've got a pretty good suspicion that if I was to make a sudden move, he could move that hand up, unsnap, draw, and fire two into my chest before I could whip out my off-duty.

Not that I intend to make any sudden move.

The other thing, that he's just casually touching his holster, well, that's by the book too. I can't complain about Sarge doing something we train people to do. Smart move.

"I'd be glad to," I say. "I'm gonna get it now."

I slowly kneel down, pull up my pants leg, and unsnap the holster on my right calf. I keep a small .38 there, 2" barrel, just for emergencies. It's a regulation: Police officers carry when off-duty.

I hold the butt by a finger and my thumb, and hold it up to him. Then I slowly raise up and take a half-step back. You're thinking that's pretty meek for a lieutenant speaking to a sergeant. But here's the thing, suppose that whoever called this in is hoping I get mad and that there's an incident, and I get shot.

Actually, that's prolly the script. I'm supposta go bat-guano on them when they find the body in my trunk, and then I get shot in the confusion. There might even be somebody looking for the chance. So me, I'm takin' it real slow, for now. I cross my arms, like I'm impatient, but mostly it's so both hands are in plain view.

Sarge, he empties my .38 into his hand and pockets the shells. The pistol goes into his other pocket. "That's the only one, right?" he asked.

"My service pistol's in my safe," I said. Well, it ain't exactly Fort Knox; it's just a lock box screwed to the shelf of my closet.

He nods to the uni, who's holding my keys. Then he backs up a bit, where he can watch me and see the trunk, both at once.

You'd think an Ell-Tee would get special treatment, and they wouldn't be watchin' me so close. But there have been some pretty high officials, even sheriffs and police chiefs, that have gone bad in this state, so there's gotta be a protocol. And Sarge is right on it.

If I wasn't an Ell-Tee, I might be cuffed in a patrol car, "for my own safety," while they do this. Except then it'd be harder for me to get shot in my fracas.

The uniform pops open the trunk lid and then takes a quick step back. It smells like stale beer.

"Spilled some beer in there," I said. "Then my laundry basket fell over. Gonna have to wash all that stuff all over again."

The CSU snapped a couple of photos, wouldn't you know, and the uniform even poked at my socks with a baton before he stepped back. He turned towards the sergeant and shook his head.

Sarge stepped over and handed me my pistol, then he reached in his other pocket and pulled out the shells. He only handed me four, and the gun takes five, but I didn't say anything to him.

Instead, I turned to the CSU. "Those pictures wind up on a bulletin board, I'll have your ass on a plaque above my desk, understand?"

He nodded. He'd have to have his Lt. give him permission to delete 'em — another protocol — but I was pretty sure he wouldn't be showing my skivvies around the office.

The uni closes the trunk and hands me my keys.

"Sorry for the confusion," he said.

"No harm done," I said, dropping my car keys back into my pants pocket. "You're just doin' the job."

The Sergeant held out his hand, and I shook it. He was just doing his job, no hard feelings.

"So, what was the complaint?" I asked. After that little act just now, they can't brush off a few questions.

"Anonymous 9-1-1," said the uni. "Said he was walkin' by, smelled decomp, knows what it smells like, called it in. Didn't want to leave a name."

"Funny thing," said the sergeant, just a bit too fast, "Some of these people, they don't know what they're smelling. I had a guy one time that called in a gas leak outside a Pizza place. Turned out it was some old garlic sauce that they threw away."

I gave him a look. "People ought to know the smell of decomp from beer."

"You'd think so," said the Sergeant.

"So when did you get this call?" I asked the uni.

He licked his lips. "It, uh, we had some other stuff to do, y'know."

"Patrol gets a little backed up sometimes," said the sergeant. "We had a 4-5-9 this morning."

"In progress?" I asked. The sergeant took a breath. "In progress, this 4-5-9?"

"No," said the uni.

"Since when do you even take a report in person on a 4-5-9?" I asked. "If they need a report for the insurance, you let 'em come to the counter, don't you?"

"Okay," said the sergeant. "Dispatch called this out around 6 AM. Maybe a little after."

"Shift change. So the guys goin' home told you, 'Yeah, you get a chance, we had a call about a smelly car

70

across the street. Might be a 1-8-7, but I gotta get home, see you tomorrow.' "

The sergeant nodded. "Look, we didn't think we'd find anything. And we didn't."

"Your boy here was gonna just pop my trunk open without a key."

"Sorry, Lieutenant, but, you know how it is, we're just doin' the job."

"You got a second call, didn't you?"

Neither one of them wanted to say anything. Look, you set somebody up, you want to see fireworks. You want to watch the stupid Ell-Tee commit suicide by cop. So whaddaya do? You call it in while he's walkin' back to his car.

So how do you know?

How do you know that he's walkin' back to his car, and how do you manage to be where you can see it, both?

I looked over at the abandoned bus station, and I scanned the roof of the old firehouse, behind me. I looked over at city hall, like I expected somebody to be hiding inside the rotunda or something. The restaurants across Gabilan Street were all dark and quiet.

I looked back at the sergeant and I thought of something.

"You know what?" I asked. "Never mind. I'm good here. You guys good here?"

They nodded and I got into my car. The uni behind me was nice enough to back up and let me out of the parking spot. When I pulled out of the lot and went right on Salinas Street, the sergeant was still chatting with him.

So what I thought was, you want to know when somebody's coming, and you want to time it so you can watch, here's what you do: You be a cop. I don't like thinking that, especially about one of Salinas' finest, but I gotta be like that Occam guy that dropped his razor. I was thinkin' that I just had a close shave.

Well, that leaves me with a basket full of problems. For one, there's a dead body out in Prunedale that was a woman who ties back to me. Sheriff will catch that one; Prunedale's unincorporated. But they'll know pretty quick I was out there talkin' to her. And they'll know pretty quick after that I used to date her sister.

'Course, a lot of people dated Glennis, over the years, and for all I know, her sister mighta been the same way. Lost touch after high school. Don't believe what Glennis said to me in the bowling alley. I didn't drink back then. Prolly got me mixed with some other bum she knew.

Second, I got somebody gunning for me. Puttin' Glennis in my trunk, then tryin' to get me shot by another cop, that's not real friendly. I mean, how often do you look in your trunk, right? Unless you got a flat tire or something.

Then I got to make some headway on a murder soon, or the Captain's gonna be up my microscope with a … that didn't come out right. You know what I mean.

And one of the open cases is Merlot. I don't exactly owe him, we did everything cash and carry. But on the other hand, he got me where I'm at. That got me thinkin' I could cash out my 457 account and go move somewhere warmer. Fresno, maybe, or San Diego. I hear it's real nice out in the Imperial Valley; Brawley maybe.

Except when they find Glennis, that'll make it look like I ran away to keep from getting' caught. Flight to escape prosecution, that's what they'll call that. So, bottom line, I got some problems.

Back in high school, hell, that was thirty years ago, maybe more, there was this guy I used to know. Real handy to talk through stuff. Always had some good ideas.

I lived off of John Street, by Sanborn, and this guy was around the curve on Williams, where the trailer park used to be. Still is. Except he prolly don't still live out there no more.

We went to Alisal High. It was a tough school even back then, and I don't mean the academics. This was not long after the North County kids got their own high school out by Castroville. Just us East-side kids, after that.

Anyway, me and Hirschman, we hung around together, tried to watch each other's back, that kinda thing. He helped me get through 11th grade history. That course coulda killed me.

So whaddaya do when you get in a hole you're too dumb to get out of? You phone a friend. Except Hirschman doesn't live in the trailer park on Williams any more, and nobody speaks English does these days. My Espan-yole is pretty awful. Cortes, in traffic, he always laughs at me and says I couldn't even order a burrito at Taco Bell. Not even if the menu had pictures.

But you know, you're back in the old neighborhood, you look around a little bit. There was a time Closter Park wasn't so bad, at least in the daytime. When I was a kid we'd play ball there and try to impress the girls. I think Hirschman's sister's best friend was sweet on me. Donna something. Think she was Irish.

That was before I met Betsy. But that's not part of this story.

Next thing I know, it's dark and I'm driving around the East Side, thinking about how it changed since I was a teenager. There's a little liquor store, corner of Garner and Alma. Been there forever. Me and ol' Hirschman, on a late Friday night, we'd go in there and buy a six-pack. Tell the clerk it was for Hirschman's old man. The clerk was usually too lit by then to check ID, or to give a rat anyway.

Just for the hell of it, I pulled up close by and went inside. It's more like a general market now, a little bit of everything. And all the signs are in Spanish. But one thing, no matter what you speak, you put a six pack on the counter and start pulling out money, they sell it to you. Works every time.

Just like that, whadda you know, I'm parked at Saint Mary Nativity, looking at the corner of Closter Park where the baskets are. I guess I oughta say the hoops, 'cause these don't even have those chain nets from when I was a kid.

If a black and white should want to know what I'm doin' in the Saint Mary parking lot, well, I'm waiting to meet an informant, and he needs to shove off so he doesn't spoil the whole deal. If there's a little beer on my breath, my gold shield ought to get me out of that one. Open container? It would take a mighty ballsy uni to cite an Ell-Tee for an open container.

So I'm sitting there sipping suds and thinking about the good ol' days when life was simple. After the third can, I told myself to back it off a little. I still gotta drive home, and while I can dodge an open container, a DUI would be a horse with different colors. I took the three empties and the three not-empties, locked 'em in my trunk, and got back in the car.

Radio was playin' eighties stuff, and that didn't hurt the mood. I'm letting the engine idle, lookin' at the b-ball courts, rememberin' old games, and wonderin' if Donna was really into me. Maybe she was just friendly. That whole thing coulda gone down a whole different road.

The bar on Alma, catty-corner from where I'm parked; the door opens and two guys come out. One's holding a paper bag with the top twisted around the neck of a bottle. You do that, it's pretty obvious what's in the bag. But people do it.

They start walking up Alma, parallel to the park, and away from me. I watch 'em for a bit – it's the cop in me, gotta see what people are doin' – but they're headed for home, looks like.

Another guy comes out, and he's not in such a hurry. He stands on the corner, then he crosses the street to where the courts are. Stands on that corner for a minute, like he's waiting for something. I'm thinking he's prolly holding and I could bust him for narcotics, except that's not my beat and if I ran him in, I'd have to explain having three beers in me.

I'm thinkin' I should get another one out of the trunk and make it four. I'm not a skinny guy. It takes a lot more alcohol to get me drunk, so a fourth wouldn't hurt. That's what I always tell myself. Might be true.

About the time I'm almost convinced to go open my trunk, I see a four-by truck coming up Alma towards the church. It's got those illegal fog-lights, like the guy's trying to be a lighthouse or something. But I'm not gonna cite him, 'cause traffic isn't my beat either. And with that much light right on me, I'm not gonna get out a beer and start sippin' it.

The driver stops at the corner, and I'm hopin' he's gonna drive off. But he's just sittin' there. The guy that was standin' around walks over beside the truck, and then he takes off running across the courts. The driver – I see him as a silhouette in his own headlight – he comes around the front of his truck and pops off a shot at the runner, then two more.

I gotta do something. I throw the car in gear, flip on the headlights, and come out of the parking lot aimed right at the truck. My idea is to pull up in front of him, whip out my service pistol and yell "Freeze!"

Problem is, I had three beers in about thirty minutes, and I'm a little bit lit. I go to stomp the brakes, and instead I hit the gas. So then I'm hoping he jumps outta the way, but he does one better. He turns and shoots right at me.

The shot goes through the windshield, and then there's a big crash and the airbag slaps me in the face. I jump out, pull my service revolver, and yell, "Police, freeze!"

Yeah, it's a little late after I already killed the guy, but I wanna make sure the witnesses heard me yell. You know there's gonna be witnesses. I checked him, and he was gone. No chance for him. But I gotta go down the list, so I call it in and ask for an ambulance.

Then I walked across the street to the bar and ordered two shots. The bartender didn't blink. He just poured two shots and plopped 'em on the bar. I threw down a twenty.

It was a might dark in there, except behind the bar. While he was making change, I poured one of the shots on the floor. There wasn't a potted plant nearby. The other one, I swirled it around in my mouth and then spit it back into the glass. When nobody was looking, it went on the floor, too. Poured 'em down the side of the bar, so they didn't splash. No big deal, the sawdust'll take it.

I stood there, leaning on the bar, holding one glass in each hand, until the uniforms arrived. I wanted them to find me in the bar, and I wanted them to report that I had just had two shots.

See, here's the thing. Cortes, he told me about a guy that did this, only they caught that guy 'cause he bragged about it. If you have a drink, they can't give you a breath test for fifteen minutes. Plus however long it takes 'em to get there. Then, they have to allow for the drinks you took.

Only I didn't really drink 'em, so instead of taking off the two shots of whiskey, they'll be subtracting two of the beers. And I got an extra fifteen minutes to work on getting my liver through the third beer. By the time they tested me and did the math, I was at about point-oh-three. That's like I had a beer with dinner a couple hours ago.

They could still do the touch your nose test and go for a DUI anyway, but one, they're not gonna do that at a crime scene, and two, they still think I just had two shots, so it wouldn't mean nothing. The Captain won't be too happy, but I won't lose my shield over it.

The story was simple, the way they seen it. I was parked at the church, tryin' to figure out how the Closter Park homicide went down. Then I witnessed this guy trying to shoot this other guy, and when I turned on my lights, he shot at me. Somebody's shootin' at you, you take 'em out. No foolin' around.

The tow truck driver took me home. Let me get the three beers outta my trunk before he towed the car off to police impound. Those three and some whiskey to chase 'em, and I slept like a baby.

I'm in the office at the crack of seven, even though I feel like my head's cracked open. I'm here to face the music. I could be the hero here, or the goat. It all depends how the wind is blowing. I'm trying to figure out if "my foot slipped off the brake" sounds better than "but I was too drunk to know where the brake was" and all that stuff like that.

Ballistics, that musta been a slow night for 'em, or else a officer-involved homicide was a big deal. They ran the bullet from my car — it was in the trunk, in a wood tool box I keep back there. Made an entrance hole for itself, knocked around some sockets and stuff, and couldn't get out the other side.

That bullet and the test bullet were both consistent with the Closter Park murder. And a guy turned up at Natividad ER with a bullet in his calf, matched all three of those. And that puts homicide at 14 for 15, not counting the guy I offed last night. Or Glennis, but she's not in our stats, and I hope to heaven she never will be.

So am I a hero for solving an outstanding murder, or am I a goat for taking out the suspect? How much holy hell can the Captain dump over me, that's the question. I don't have to wait long. He walks in while I'm pretending to look at the morning reports. Cortes is with him.

"Licowicz, gimme your gun and shield," he said. I looked up at him like I didn't see him come in. Cortes is looking kinda sheepy, like he doesn't want to be part of this, but he's got no choice.

"Morning, Captain," I said, sliding my badge and my service pistol across the desk.

"Yeah," he said. "Sergeant Cortes is gonna be running your people while you're on suspension. Give him a quick rundown on what's going on, then get the hell out of here. We'll call you when we want you." And I'm pretty sure when the Captain will want me is gonna be the second never of next week.

"Sure," I said.

The Captain walked out, leaving me and Cortes there. I pointed to a chair. He sat down.

"Sorry about this," he said. "You know how it is."

"It's not you," I said. "It's how it is." I shrugged. "So as of this morning, we've got one open murder. It's a guy name of Chris Merlot, got himself stabbed in the eye with an icepick. Some sort of fight over a bill."

"A day of reckoning," nodded Cortes.

"Yeah. So, I knew this guy. Normally, me and Sanchez, we woulda talked it out, and I woulda had her following the leads. But I guess you heard, she went to major case.

"I been out to try an talk to his girlfriend. I seen 'em together, and I knew her from some prior stuff. You remember that meth lab that blew up out in Prunedale, couple years back?"

"That woman?" His eyes got big. "I remember her from Peterson in narcotics talking about it. Said she was buzzing around like a hornet. They had to wait three days to get a statement."

"Well, she was married to a meth cook. Anyway, I went out and talked to her once. Tried again a second time, but nobody was home. And I saw her downtown once, talked briefly, she wanted to make a fight out of it."

"You get anything out of her?"

"She said he was gonna talk to somebody named Bill. No, wait, he was gonna see someone about a bill, like a tab." I scratched my head. "I shoulda been takin' notes. Yeah, when she left him and went home, he was gonna see somebody."

"Not with an icepick in his eye. Any other leads?"

"I had a thing with a tattoo, shown it to Sundaram, but he hasn't gotten back to me yet. Like tic-tac-toe, only just X, no O. Three of 'em, but not in a row."

"Anything else?"

"Only other open right now just got hit by a car. I think that one's gonna come back as justified. Maybe even good police work." I got up and put my hands on my hips. "Call me if you got questions," I said. "Or Sanchez. She's real good with this stuff."

I walked away, went out the back, where the squad cars are. Cortes, he's a good guy, even if he spells his name funny. Told him it should have a Z on the end, he says he's not Mexican, he's Brazilian. It's a Portagee thing. Whatever.

When I get out back, I see Sanchez and another sergeant having a chat over by the ramp that goes down under city hall. I raise my chin, like a nod, and she does the same. And just then my phone chimes, like I got a new message.

The other sergeant piped up.

"It's the Jet Propulsion Laboratory," he said. "They want to know how much rocket fuel it takes to get to Mars."

"How the hell would I know?" I ask.

Sanchez stared at him and her face got red. "You're showing Uranus," she said. "And it ain't pretty." That's when I got the joke. Yeah, how the hell would I know.

"Just joking," he said, but I cut him off.

"You didn't mean nothing, didja Pal? So why don't you give me a chance to talk to my friend here, and you get a cup of coffee inside?" He took my hint and went into the station.

"Listen," I said to Sanchez, "Thanks for that, but don't take no heat on account of me. I'm like a cat. No matter how you drop me, I got nine lives left."

She gave me a grin that was more worried than happy. "You take care of yourself."

"Don't worry about me. I'm good. Little vacation, catch up on the soaps."

"Want a lift home?"

"I'm tryin' to walk more these days. You know, to keep my figure."

I did walk towards home, and I got as far as the liquor store on Clay Street. Little hair-off-the-dog, so I'd be able to go back to sleep once I got home. I picked up a couple paper bags, and I didn't twist the bags around the necks of what was in 'em.

I'm not really sure if I got home or not.

I woke up on a couch.

It wasn't my couch.

I was wearing my clothes.

Wearing my clothes was good. It meant I knew where my clothes were. There's been times I wasn't even this lucky. I checked my pockets, and everything was supposed to be in 'em was in 'em. All things considered, not a bad start.

I started to get up, and that wasn't such a good idea.

I wondered if I still had something to drink. Wasn't sure what, but it might fix the blown fuses in my head and the nausea in my gut. And the thirst. My mouth was like, I dunno, a desert or something.

Had to get something to drink, yeah, the bottles. If there was anything still in 'em, a shot or two would go good.

Found my way to the kitchen.

One of the bottles I bought was empty. Not a drop in it, and it was some cheap stuff, anyway. Prolly why I had a headache, drinkin' awful stuff like that. Smells like varnish, and don't taste much better.

The other stuff was good, a name brand, but I'm not gonna tell you the name. Starts with a J, if that helps you.

There was a little at the bottom, maybe a couple ounces. Enough for a shot. It was sittin' in the sink, like somebody was gonna rinse out the bottles later. Can't have 'em stinkin' for the trash man, right?

I looked for a glass, but they wasn't where I woulda put 'em, so I gave up and drank it straight outta the bottle. I guess it helped.

Now, where the hell was I?

I rinsed the bottle and drank some tap water out of it, since I couldn't find any glasses. It tasted like Salinas water, hard as cement. But it was cold and wet and I prolly chugged a third of a bottle of the stuff.

There was a calendar over the stove, and somebody pinned a bill to it. The bill was addressed to Christopher Merlot, 311 West Winham Street.

Okay, so I didn't get far from the liquor store. Probably went to the park by Clay and Capitol, started sipping from the paper bags. Like I said, that don't fool nobody. And nine, ten in the morning, people are gonna see that. Maybe even cops.

So I would've started home, maybe gone a block down to Winham Street, and started to walk east. And that would've brought me here, Merlot's place. But how did I know it was Merlot's place, and how did I get in?

Just in case, I got both bottles, took 'em to the sink, and washed 'em real good. Even the mouths, in case I was sippin' straight from the bottle. Since there weren't no glasses, that was a good bet.

I put 'em both in the sink and then I looked around real good. I didn't want to find Glennis in the bedroom or nothing like that, you know what I mean. Well, I was alone, and there wasn't any sign of nobody else bein' there since Merlot died. My people would've had the landlord let 'em in to look for clues, but they wouldn't have been back since.

There was a keyring on the stand by the door. Two keys on it. One of them had a number stamped on it, 27633. I found my notebook and wrote that down. That and a good locksmith, I could have me a key if I ever needed it.

I checked, and that key opened the door. I put it back where I found it and made sure I didn't leave fingerprints.

There weren't any scratch marks around the keyhole, so I didn't pick the lock, and all my tools for that are at my place, under my mattress. Or I guessed that they were, because they weren't in none of my pockets. So how did I get in?

I went to the library, to use one a their computers. They make you give up your driver's license. I got one where I could work for a while and nobody bother me, and I started looking for Hirschman. I found where his sister got married. I found where he got interviewed about a robbery at an Italian place on highway 68 that ain't there no more. And that was it. Not another word about him.

So I looked for the sister, and like a lot of folks who grew up in Salinas, her and her husband moved to L.A. I got a number for them, but it was disconnected. Dead end all the way around.

Well, that got me looking for Donna. She was Irish, and it was one of those names that you hear it and you think Irish right away. Not like mine, people think I'm maybe German or Russian or something.

So I started with every Irish name I could think of, and it come up under Donnally. Yeah, like I couldn't remember Donna Donnally. Did I mention I'm not the sharpest knife? Still, I shoulda remembered that quicker.

What I'm seeing is, she graduated nursing school and got a job at the hospital. Natividad, not Memorial. Well, good for her. She had a brother that worked himself ragged keeping her in school, which is prolly why he did so bad in school.

I was startin' to want something more like breakfast, so I traded the computer for my driver's license and got outta there. Figured I'd go home, get some eggs, take a shower, maybe go watch the ball game down at the bowling alley. Problem is, I'm walking down Pine Street, and a black and white goes by, lights only. Pulls up with some other black and whites about a block away.

Well, that wasn't real good, 'cause it looked like it was by my apartment building. Then I started thinkin', what if somebody put Glennis in my apartment? The trunk didn't work, so they went for something a bit more obvious.

I turned around and started casually strolling up Pajaro. Me bein' on suspension and all, what's going on there is none of my business until I find out that it was my business. I turned on Oak, and that put me pretty well out of plain sight. Then my phone dinged. Text message.

Scared the hell outta me, to be honest. Didn't realize I was so jumpy till then. Coffee and breakfast woulda done me well.

I looked at it. It was from Cortes. He went to Prunedale to see if he could talk to Glennis about the Merlot murder. Pounded on her door, but nobody was home. Wanted to know if I knew where else she could be.

Try the liqour stor I sent, but typing with my thumbs, I got the o and the u wrong. I was hoping he didn't smell something wrong and go in. The longer before she got found, the better.

There was another text on my phone, prolly the one I got when I was talking to Sanchez behind the PD. That's the police station, if you didn't know. It was from Sundaram. I figured I'd ignore it for now.

I got breakfast at a fast food place on Main Street. Not my first choice, cause the only way they do eggs is to scramble 'em up and put 'em in something. Burritos,

84

muffins, rolled up pancakes. I like mine fried. In a restaurant I always say "Over medium." Plus, the stuff those fast food places call coffee... I won't tell you how bad it is. You prolly know.

While I was sitting there, I saw two more cars go down Pine, lights only. Whatever was going on at my apartment – well, maybe it was only near my apartment. Maybe they finally decided to bust that house across the street. Cars coming and going all night long – if that's not a cat house, I'm in the wrong business.

No, Murphy's law, the cars gotta all be going to my place. Whatever's gonna go wrong, is gonna go wrong. Cortes has something funny he says about that, like it wasn't really Murphy, it was that other guy. Whatever that means.

Well, I figure I'll find out about it when they call me and ask me to come in. Showin' up there would be settin' myself up to get shot or something. So now what? I can't go home, and I still feel awful from last night.

Well, I start walking back to the library, thinkin' I'll maybe use the computers some more, and then figure it out. Then I said to myself, Merlot had a computer, right? In fact, he had a computer that printed that picture of me, kneeling over Glennis. And that picture with the icepick in somebody's hand.

So what if that same computer's got more pictures?

There's a locksmith on Gabilan. He gave me a little grief that I couldn't tell him what brand of key, but finally I looked at the blank ones and pointed to the one I wanted. He cut it to the numbers I gave him, but he told me if it didn't work he wasn't gonna take it back. Fair enough, I guess.

The locksmith is right next to the Brass Rail, so I thought a beer might be a good chaser for my late breakfast, plus I'd been walkin' a lot. Build up a thirst that way. One beer couldn't hurt me, right? Not like I'm gonna drive home.

I was on my third beer when Sanchez walked in. She looked around, saw me at the bar, and walked over.

"Let's grab a table," she said.

I took my beer and followed her to a small booth at the end, where we were two or three tables from anybody.

"You want something?" I asked, raising my hand for the bartender. He didn't see me.

"No," she said, motioning for me to put my hand down. "Look, I'm not here. I was in your office, and I spotted this on the desk." She slid a paper across to me, folded three times like a letter. I unfolded it and glanced at it. Me and Glennis.

"I can explain," I said, in a loud whisper.

"Forget it," she said. "But somebody knows that you were at Cortes' crime scene this morning, and got this picture of you. And they tried to give it to Cortes. I don't know if he saw that."

"It's not what you think," I said.

"Oh, so you didn't listen to the radio, hear about a body in Prunedale, and slip into the crime scene?"

"Prunedale? That's not us … Shouldn't that be the Sheriff's problem?"

"Yeah, but Cortes was first on scene and he told 'em it was related to that Merlot guy you were always talking about. So he got control of the scene." She looked around. "I'm late to another DB, a shooting over off California Street, if you can believe that."

"Really? I always thought that was a real nice neighborhood." It used to be, you know.

"You never know," she said. "There's something weird about it they won't say on the radio. Weird enough to call in Major Case." She looked around and then stood up. "Wait at least ten minutes after I leave before you leave, okay? I don't want anyone thinking I tipped you about the Prunedale thing."

"I'll go out the back way," I said, but I was talking to her back.

I did go out the back, and made my way west and south, just not very steady either way.

I let myself into Merlot's place. It was just the way I left it, so I took a nap on the couch.

It was dark when I woke up. I turned on a light. It was about ten-thirty by the clock on Merlot's desk. The desk made me think of the computer, and sure enough there was a laptop there, and it was connected to a printer. There was another cable plugged into it, too, went to a big box thing beside the desk.

I was trying to figure out what the box thing was. It had some little lights on the front, and one of those display things on the front, and some other pieces and parts that made no sense to me.

As I'm watching it, the display lights up, and there's a bleep sound. Prolly some kinda fax machine, and it prolly got a fax. I'm looking around for paper coming out, but I just see numbers on the front, counting down from 1200. So I shrugged and opened up the laptop. It has a screen, black and white like a chalkboard, that says, "Enter the security key."

"What security key?" I said it out loud, cause I don't see nothing that looks like a key, or a keyhole to stick it in.

Meanwhile, this little box is making a bleep sound every time the numbers go down another hundred, like 1100, 1000, 900... I can't think with it doing that. I was tempted to unplug it, but I didn't want to break something.

I went into the kitchen to see if I could find a beer, or something stronger. I found one beer in the fridge, so I brought it back into the living room. Now the little box thing is making that bleep every fifty, like 650, 600, 550. At 500, it starts bleeping every twenty, then at 300, it's bleeping every ten. At 60, I'm thinking that there's just a minute to go, so I polish off the beer and put the bottle down on the desk.

Maybe when it gets to zero, it'll stop and maybe it'll unlock the laptop. But after sixty, it's bleeping every second. At five, it's bleeping two, maybe three times a second.

I know, you figured it out already. Me, it takes till it hits five before I realize that it's a bomb. As I'm yanking the cords out of the laptop and running for the door, there's orange-brown smoke pouring out the sides of this little box. I can't get a break today.

I pulled an alarm as I went down the hallway, but nothing happened, so I yelled "FIRE," as loud as I could. About then, Merlot's smoke alarms start going off, and I left the door open, so I start to hear other voices, and people shouting. I kept running till I was out the door and on the street.

Folks are coming out of the building now, and I see lights coming on in the windows. For a second I'm thinking it was my fault, but the box started doing that stuff before I touched the laptop. I think Merlot musta had it rigged, where if he didn't put in a code, it would burn up. Maybe every 30 days, cause that's about how long it was between Merlot dying and the box catching fire.

Right about the time I'm thinking that, the big horns on the side of the building go off, like it took that long for the fire alarm to realize that somebody pulled the little lever. I saw people on cell phones, and then, downtown, I could hear sirens. Prolly first thing, a cop car is gonna show up. I didn't want to run away, 'cause the first thing you learn when you're a cop is you see somebody running away, they're the one caused the problem. I don't wanna be that guy. Too many things to answer right now.

I moved to the back of the people there, where I got people between me and the building. There was a lot of smoke, and it was white smoke, like the wood's on fire. I kept moving around the back of the crowd, and next thing I knew, I was all the way back to the cross street, Lincoln.

That end of Lincoln don't go nowhere. It's just a little stub that goes to the high school parking lot. And there's a couple of small streets that connect it to South Main. So I slipped a little farther down the street, then turned around and started casually walking away. Just a man taking his laptop for a walk, getting' some fresh air, in a free country where it's perfectly legal to do that.

I crossed Main, and next thing I knew my little feet were leading me home. The squad cars were gone, but there was a yellow X of caution tape across one door. I knew without looking that it said "Police Line, Do Not Cross." Looks like my apartment was a crime scene. And they got one of them things goes over a doorknob and has a padlock on it.

On the back stairs, there's a window with an iron rail outside of it. If you step over that rail, you know, so you're facing the window from the outside, you can side-step to a rail that's on the bedroom window of my apartment. I know that 'cause I get locked out some time. It happens, okay? And I never said I was Einstein, did I? Alright then.

Anyway, long story short, I was in my own apartment, just like that. It looked tore up a little. I think some of my buddies from the force were in here making a mess of the place. In the front room, I seen why. There was a bullet hole in my floor, and a dark red stain around makes me think of blood.

There was knife marks around the hole, like they dug out the bullet to match it up.

Just the one bullet hole, but from the blood stains, I guess one's all you need, right? So that kinda pissed me off more than seeing my stuff scattered by the police. Them I could understand; they was doing their job. The part that pissed me off was that two people was in here first, and one of them shot the other.

Of course I wanted to know what happened, so I turned on the TV real low and checked the couch for bloodstains. I didn't see nothing, so I sat down. Of course the news is past all the headlines, so there won't be nothing. They woulda reported a murder at the top of the hour, especially at a cop's house.

I turned on my computer, a big old clunky thing, but I can't find nothing on any websites either. I keep searching for "Salinas shooting" but I get stuff that's really old, like last year, or stuff that's going on in Peru. See, that's what I hate about computers. You put in Salinas, and they think, maybe he don't mean Salinas, he means Peru. What the hell, right?

Anyway, the TV's yammering behind me and I hear them say, "Apartment Fire in South Salinas." South Salinas means everything south and west of the 100 block of Main, so I look to see where it was. I dunno if it was the beers — I had a couple after I climbed in the window — or me just being stupid, but until I seen it on TV, I forgot about setting Merlot's place on fire.

So I leave the computer and watch the TV. Sure enough, that's the place, and there's a lot of smoke, firemen walking around with hoses, you name it. The guy yammerin' over the video is saying that somebody saw two teenagers running out the door with a laptop just before the alarms went off.

Funny, 'cause I didn't see 'em. Only person with a laptop I saw was me. Then they was sayin' that Merlot's place was totaled, the place below him was damaged, nobody was hurt, and the fire is rumored to have started in a toaster.

They showed the firemen carryin' out that black box I told you about. Toaster, sure. Might as well call it a toaster. Beats the hell outta me what else it coulda been.

About then my cell phone dings. Not the cop cell phone, the other one that I keep for personal stuff. I check the text messages and there's one from Glennis. Yeah, somebody told me this joke, it goes, "Man, it sure is hot here. See you on Tuesday." It's kinda like that, right?

The message said, *Where R U ? need 2 twlk.*

Right. Glennis needs to talk to me. But who would send that to me? It's gotta be from the guys that iced her. *Who is this?*

Gle – I dunno what they were gonna do, tell me it was Glennis, like I didn't know she was dead? Or try to get me to meet 'em alone somewhere, like in a TV show. But they just sent me the three letters, and that was it.

I'm thinking it was a bad idea coming back to my place. They might come back to follow up on the crime scene. Or they might figure I'd come here, and come to try and get me.

Stupid people do stupid stuff, and that's how most criminals get caught. So sleeping in my own bed was a really bad idea. But three more beers and a shot of whiskey, and I slept there anyway.

Phone's ringing. I know it's ringing because my head hurts when it rings. I grab it off the nightstand and answer it. "Yellow?"

"Ice Ice Baby," said Cortes.

"Same to you," I said, and started to hang up. I hear him yelling at the phone. I put it back to my ear. "Whaddaya want?"

"Licowicz, listen, we need to talk. Any chance you can come down here and make a statement?"

"About what?"

"About what. I gotta give it to you, Earl, you're cool as ice. Must be why you always answer the phone like that, right?"

"Look, I'm on suspension, which is like a vacation except it don't come off my vacation days. So tell me what you want or get off my phone."

"Dude, chill, right? This is Miguel you're talkin' to. I wouldn't normally do it, but I gotta ask you a few questions. Captain's on my back to get you down here so you can give us a little insight on how that guy got into your apartment."

"What guy?"

"The dead guy."

"There's a dead guy? In my apartment?"

"Not any more, he's in the morgue. Come on, Earl, don't make me do this the hard way."

"Look, Cortes. Nothin' personal, but if there was a dead guy in my apartment, and you want me to make a statement, here's the statement. I want my lawyer. So when I find my lawyer, I'll give you a call about me maybe making a statement."

"You're lawyering up?" He said it like it was a personal slap in the face or something.

"575-6163," I said. "Chance Franklin." I still got one of them big old phone books next to my bed. Never got around to throwin' it out. While Cortes was yammerin', I flipped it open and stuck my finger on an ad for a lawyer.

"Okay," he said, with that tone like, *if that's how you want it.* He hung up and the display went back to normal. And I noticed I still got one text message, from that day I saw Sanchez out behind the police station. It was the one from Sundaram. I opened it up and it said *Tattoo you asked about – found a guy who fits that – out of town talent – freelance muscle for a company from Arizona. Might be tied to org crime.*

Alright, so now I had a lead on Merlot, and I was a pretty popular guy. The cops wanted to talk to me, and so did Merlot's dead girlfriend. So should I go to the station first, or the morgue?

While I was laughing about all the folks who wanted to talk to me all of a sudden, I made some eggs and bacon, and I brewed some coffee. When I was done, I did a few other things you only do at home, because if I went to the station and talked to Cortes, I might not be home again for a while. Maybe a long time.

I got a shower, which was nice, 'cause I didn't feel right showering at Merlot's place. Too vulnerable, just too weird. And I might not get a chance again soon, so I enjoyed a nice long shower.

Speaking of Chance, I called that lawyer.

When I got to the station, Cortes hustled me into a small triangle room. We've got these rooms, there's four of 'em. They used to be two small rooms, with doors on each end. The big brass decided we needed four tiny rooms instead of two small ones. So they added two kitty-corner walls, and put in some of those one-way windows.

The one we was in, it had one a them old payphones in it, looked it been through a war. I suppose it was so you could call a lawyer, or else dial-a-prayer. I dunno if it worked. I bet not. Looked like maybe crazy people been usin' it to crack walnuts.

The rooms, they got little tables in 'em, and two chairs, and that's all you can fit into there. It's that tiny. Three people max. Even just me, waiting, I was startin' to feel closet-phobic.

Finally Cortes opens the door, and he's got some guy in a suit. Makes me think of that guy used to sing with that woman, then he got in a skiing accident, they got divorced first – I think he was in politics or something. The guy's real thin, and he's taller than that singer. But they could be, I dunno, cousins maybe.

"I'm Chance Franklin," he said. "We spoke on the phone earlier."

"Right," I said. "This guy here is Miguel Cortes. Used to be a buddy of mine. Took over my office when I got suspended."

"Yes, you remarked on that," said Chance, giving Cortes a look. I liked the guy already, even if he was eating up my retirement. If you don't know what it costs to hire a lawyer in a criminal case, I'm happy for you.

"So, Mr. Cortes," said Chance, "Is this meeting being recorded?"

"Well, yes," he said. "It's the way we do it." He looked at me like I shoulda known that. I did. Still, lawyers ask silly questions. It's what you pay them to do. "Now first thing, Earl, I've gotta read you something. You have the right…"

"Before you do that," said Chance, "I'm also recording this meeting." He pulled out his cell phone,

94

tapped on the screen a few times, and put it down on the table, right between me and Cortes.

Cortes looked at it, then he started again. "You have the right to remain silent. Anything you do say can be used against you in court. You have the right to have an attorney present during questioning. If you cannot afford an attorney, one will be appointed for you without charge. Do you understand these rights?"

"He does," said Chance.

"Do you wish to waive these rights?"

"He does not," said Chance. Cortes put a paper and a pen in front of me. Chance took them, initialed the paper, and handed it back to Cortes.

"Alright, so Earl – Elton Earl Licowicz – You are being questioned as a suspect in the murder of one Jaime Jorge Rosales, of 332B Acosta Plaza." He paused, like he wanted me to say something. He pronounced the name Hymie Hor-Hay, by the way, not Jamie George like I woulda said.

"So, Earl, just what exactly was this guy doing in your apartment?"

"My client does not know, and assumes that Mister Rosales broke into my client's apartment."

"How do we know Earl didn't let him in?"

"You have Earl's word on it."

"So how did you know him?" asked Cortes, turning his eyes back on me.

"My client is unaware of any acquaintance with any individual named Jaime Rosales."

"Well, that's a problem," said Cortes. "'Cause Jaime wound up dead on his floor."

"My client denies knowledge of the incident."

"Do you always let people you don't know into your apartment? Do you find bodies there often?"

"My client didn't know that Mr. Rosales was in his apartment. Much less dead."

"I find that mighty convenient," said Cortes, "Since Rosales was shot with a gun just like the one Earl's got strapped to his ankle. Speakin' of which, Earl, you mind givin' that up?"

Chance nodded to me, so I slowly bent down and unstrapped the whole ankle holster. Laid it on the table. Aside from doin' that one thing, I was bein' still and quiet as one of them wooden nickels used to be in drugstores.

Cortes took it out of the holster and dumped out the bullets. There were only four rounds in it, 'cause that's all I put back after the parking lot thing with my trunk, and people lookin' for Glennis. Cortes sniffed the gun. I thought people only did that on TV.

Then he put the bullets into his pants pocket, and the gun into the other.

"You carryin' anything else?" he asked.

"No," said Chance, "And we'll need a receipt for that gun and those four rounds."

"Sure," said Cortes. "Serial number WX-42253, .38 caliber, revolver, Windsor-American Arms model 5WX."

"So noted."

"Gun does not smell of burned powder or show signs of recent discharge."

"Also noted."

"Rounds are stamped with the logo of Free State Arms, factory loads, primers intact, .38 Special. Quantity of unfired rounds is 4."

"Further noted."

Cortes reached down into one of them big vanilla envelopes, and pulled out an evidence bag. It was sealed with a big red seal across the top. Down in the bottom there was a single shell.

"We found this spent casing at Earl's apartment. Any comment on that?"

"How do you know that Mr. Rosales didn't bring it there himself?"

"Because it has Earl's fingerprint on it. Plus it's Freestate Arms, factory loaded, just like the ones in Earl's gun just now."

"That could have happened any number of ways."

"Name one."

"Mr. Licowicz might have unloaded one of his guns for some reason, put the rounds away in a safe and lawful manner, and then Mr. Rosales may have stolen the round and loaded it into his own pistol. Which was later used to kill him."

"Or Earl used it to shoot Rosales, then emptied his gun so he could clean it, and put back the four unused rounds. The empty casing he dropped onto the floor."

"That's a theory of the crime," said Chance, "But it would be just as reasonable to think that my client was emptying his gun after a day at the range, and dropped one shell onto the floor. It could have lain there for months. Unless you intend to demonstrate that he has his apartment cleaned twice weekly – which he doesn't – that's reasonable doubt."

"What about the fact that we found it in a gun, at the crime scene, next to the dead body?"

"Well, that changes the perspective."

"What if it was the gun that killed Rosales?"

"Was it?"

"Ballistics says so."

"Then I'll need to confer with my client to get an answer for you. You'll have to stop your recorder, of course."

"Let's come back to that. See, we have an interesting little theory of how this all went down."

"By all means, amuse me," said Chance.

"Earl wasn't out at Closter Park to get perspective on the old unsolved case. Think about it. Homicide is batting 13 out of 15 so far this year. He could go the rest of the year without closing a case, and he'd beat Chicago, New York, and Houston by miles.

"But Earl's got two open cases, and he's going to go to a case with no witnesses and no evidence, and he's gonna sit around in case he gets lucky and finds a clue. And lo and behold, he catches and conveniently kills a suspect holding the murder weapon.

"And that suspect happens to have wounded a guy, who winds up dead in Licowicz apartment."

"Lucky for him," said Chance. "That he was in the right place at the right time to solve that one case. But luck's not illegal."

"No, but homicide is. How about we tell the story this way: He's out by Closter Park to make a drug buy. His dealer wants more money. So Earl says it's in his car. He goes to the car, starts it up, rams the dealer. Then he jumps out, yells for the guy to freeze, and fires a shot into his own car. Passerby sees this, runs across the Park to get away, and Earl shoots him in the calf. Then he puts the murder gun on the dead dealer, and gets himself a drink to celebrate."

"Why did he yell for the guy to freeze after he had already jumped out? The suspect was already dead."

"Confuse the witnesses. Did they hear him shout for the guy to freeze? Well, yes, they heard all that. Just too late, is all."

"What happened to the drugs?"

"Wound up in the pocket of the passerby. Aside from a couple people who heard the crash and ran to see what happened after it all happened, the only witness is the passerby. Who got shot at Earl's place. So that sounds like maybe Earl doesn't want people to know what really happened."

"Quite a good story," said Chance. "Do they all live happily ever after?"

"The only one still living is Earl, and sad to say, he might not be very happy when it's all over."

"One other thing that just occurred to me: The gun you say was recovered at my client's apartment – were his fingerprints on any of the other rounds?"

"There were no other rounds," said Cortes. "Just that one casing."

"Great," said Chance. "That'll be no problem at all then. When would you like my client to come in for arraignment? Or would you prefer to drop this charade right now?"

"Are you kidding me? Are you kidding me?" Cortes' eyeballs looked like they was gonna pop outta his head. His face was red like, I dunno, a tomato or something. Then he stopped, held up one finger, and did one of those breathing things, where they close their eyes for a second. Some yoga thing, maybe.

"Listen," said Cortes, when his eyes come open again. "The DA still hasn't decided if he's going for vehicular homicide in the other case. It could go either way. There's a witness out in Prunedale who died just like that Merlot guy, and come to find out, she's an old friend of his. People around him find themselves dead. So far, his C.I., the C.I.'s girlfriend who was almost his sister-in-law, a guy trying to buy drugs at Closter Park, and the guy he tried to buy from. And that last one died in Earl's living room.

"The rat squad wants to take your client apart with a dull spoon. Did I mention that there's this guy, dead, in his apartment? Like it or not, Earl is going away for a long time. This is California, and we've got the ninth circus court, so I'm pretty safe sayin' he's not getting the gas chamber. Or at least not for a long time."

He sighed, and then kept going. "But honest, Earl, as much as I hate the idea, I've got to send you to prison for the rest of your life. I've gotta do right by all the people you killed."

"While we commend your devotion to duty," said Chance, "My client is not guilty of murder, and if you thought about it for a second, you'd see that."

Cortes didn't say anything, but his forehead wrinkled up. Long story short, him and my lawyer yammered some more, and then I walked out. Well, me and Chance. Well, they got somebody from the DAs office down there, too, and the three of them stepped into the hallway, because there wasn't any more space in that tiny little room. Get a fourth person in there and we wouldn't had any air.

There was some yelling, somebody got really mad, and then Chance came back in and got me. And we walked right out the front door. Say what you will about lawyers, but I got my money's worth.

There's a diner in Moss Landing, called the Moss Landing Diner. Yeah, they get real smart with the names out there. It's supposed to look like it was a train car once. It's on a road with too many R's in it. I wanna say Portero or Protero but them ain't right. Whatever. Look on the map, you wanna know.

Anyway, that's where I am, on that road, in the diner. You got Highway 1, you got the liquor store on the corner, and then you got this diner. And sittin' in a booth, eatin' burnt pancakes and staring across the street at the artichokes, you got me.

Actually, dark as it's getting, I'm not really staring at the artichokes. Just into the dark where the field is. One other thing you should know: I'm wearing a wire. Chance set it up with Cortes, said I should go there and then call the Captain. So I did.

I'm on my second cup of coffee, and I'm taking my time with the pancakes. This could be a long night. I start looking at the cars in front, just for somethin' to think about besides people that want me dead.

There's a red Volkswagen right in front, looks like somebody made it into a dune buggy. Between the diner and the liquor store, there's a small white pickup, backed in with the bed towards the diner. One of them imports. It's got three bags of concrete and one of them big metal washtubs. Somebody's doin' their own sidewalk, prolly.

There's another pickup, fire engine red, with a camper shell, parked at the other end of the diner. I figure that's the cook; I think I seen it here before. Me, I had somebody drop me off at the liquor store.

I was startin' to think I shoulda gone inside and got some whiskey to make this coffee taste better. It was bitter as ... it was real bitter. And it's got that taste like it was on the burner too long.

Then I realized something. Somethin' wrong about that little white truck. That concrete might not be for somebody's sidewalk. The wrong kind. Sets up too fast. Before I was a cop, I worked a lot of summers helping do concrete work. I don't know much, but I know a little about concrete.

I whistled for the waitress – she went in the back about ten minutes before – and when she stuck her head outta the kitchen, I held up my mug. She gave me a look and then brought me some more coffee.

While she was pouring, I said, "Could you bring some more sugar? This one's all out." I hold up the little plastic holder. All it's got is pink and blue and yellow and green – all the cutesy colors 'cept plain ol' sugar. There's one of them big shaker things, too. It's empty too.

She grabbed the glass sugar shaker thing, slammed it on the next booth over, and gave me the one from that booth. It was maybe half full. I looked at my coffee cup and wondered if it would be enough.

"Anything else?" she snapped. Her face was askin' if my leg was broke, I couldn't get up for the other shaker. I added her to the list of people prolly wanted to kill me.

I shook my head, like no, I'm good. She dint have to be so snippy. So much for her tip, you know?

She vanishes again, and I started into the pancakes, hoping to get 'em mostly finished before company arrived. That was maybe ten minutes.

The sergeant showed up first; the one from the parking lot, that day when my trunk didn't have a dead body in it. He walked in, looked around, and walked over to my booth. Slid in across from me. If the waitress heard him come in, she didn't show any sign of it. Just me and the sergeant in the place. I gave him a warm smile. I decided to just call him Sarge.

"I knew you'd be one of them," I said. "It was that little magic trick you did with my gun. All five rounds went into your pocket, and only four come out. So where did number five go? Well, we'd need to ask Mr. Rosales, wouldn't we?"

"You might as well take off the wire," he said. "The recorder it goes to got broken. Right now, Cortes is listening to the ball game. He thinks it's on the overhead speakers in here."

"I'd offer you coffee or something, but the waitress seems to be busy in the kitchen. I think she hates me."

"Yeah," said Sarge. "Fact is, there's a problem out back, namely, a police officer who's telling the cook and the waitress to hide out in the cooler, and to forget anybody was ever here."

"That would be the guy that was talking to Sanchez that one day. The guy made the joke about me and rocket fuel." I took another bite of pancakes and spilled some syrup. It dripped on my sock.

"Two for three," he said. "We tried to get Sanchez to give us some dirt on you, but she wouldn't play. Care to guess the third? No, you probably don't know him. He's not a cop."

"Then I prolly don't know him," I said. "Hey, can you pass the syrup from that other booth? This one's empty." I held up the little glass dispenser.

"Pancakes. That's what you're having for your last meal?" He didn't take his eyes off me, so I couldn't clock him with it, and he didn't reach for the other table.

"Well, as long as I thought Cortes was coming in to save the day, I didn't think this was my last meal."

"Sorry to break the news, but Cortes is gonna get a call in a minute to break off the operation, because they saw you and a bottle of whiskey wander off into that artichoke field across the street. Which means you've got a terminal disease."

"A who?"

"You're walking around dead already and you just don't know it yet."

"That's pretty bad," I said, forking another big square of pancakes. Not that bad, even bein' burnt. A little bit too sweet, maybe. "I thought I was feelin' fine."

A guy walked in from the kitchen, and Sarge was right. I didn't know him. He came over and stood at the end of the table. He leaned on his fingertips. The place between his thumb and his first finger, on his right hand, he had a faint tattoo. It was a tic-tac-toe match that somebody didn't know how to play.

Behind him was that other sergeant, the one thought I got calls from NASA.

"So where's the laptop?" said Sarge.

"What laptop? This got somethin' to do with that one toaster?"

"What toaster?" asked NASA.

"That thing started the fire at Merlot's place."

"Oh," said Sarge. "Yeah. Humphrey here came all the way from Tucson to get it. Seems it was stolen from a company he works for down there."

I looked at the guy with the tattoo. Guess he was Humphrey. Too bad the wire wasn't gettin' all this.

"Merlot stole it?"

"And used it, and rigged it to catch fire if he didn't enter the code every 30 days." said Sarge.

NASA coughed. "Time to go," said he said. "All secure in the back." Sarge nodded toward the door.

"You guys couldn't make another?"

Humphrey shook his head. "Stole the only plans too, the little rat bastard. Plus, he was usin' it, and we couldn't have that."

"So you stabbed him in the eye."

"Yeah. That's what we do with blackmailers." He took my arm, to pull me up.

"I got this," I said, sliding out. I shook my legs to make sure my pants legs was hiding my socks. I threw a couple twenties on the table, which woulda left over a big tip. What the hell, service wasn't that bad, and if these guys had their way, I wouldn't need money.

"So, here's the thing," said Sarge, as NASA and Humphrey took my arms, "If you've got the laptop, and if it's got the plans on it, we got orders to just shoot you. If you don't, then we've gotta do things the hard way. The four of us take a walk on the beach, and only three of us come back."

"Cause my shoes are too heavy, right?"

"You got it on the first try," said NASA. "You might not be so dumb after all."

"Don't call me dumb," I said. "It's like a insult to people can't talk." They laughed.

People always said that to me, so I figured anything that stalled them, it's worth sayin'. Sarge, he jumps in the white pickup. He looks around for traffic, and zooms off up the road. Me and my two bodyguards, we just walk.

"So, to be clear, you don't have the laptop, right?" said Humphrey.

"Dunno nothing about a laptop."

"Too bad," said NASA, with that smart-ass tone like it ain't really too bad.

We get down to the parking lot by the beach, and the little white truck is sitting there. The washtub and the concrete ain't there no more.

"Hey," I said, "You guys mind if I kick off my shoes?" They don't say nothing, so I use the toe of one shoe to pull my foot outta the other, and then I switch. "Those are my good shoes. Hate to see 'em get ruined."

"What size are you?" asks NASA.

"12 most of the time."

"Too big," he said. We start trudging over the dune and down towards the water. They got flashlights, 'cause it's black out there.

Sarge is down by the surf, and he's pouring water from a bucket. Then he's got a shovel, and he's mixing up the washtub.

When I walk up, he pulls a gun and motions to the washtub. I'm thinking, what, I don't let you kill me slow, you're gonna kill me fast? Then I think there's a lot of places you could shoot somebody, won't kill 'em. But it'll make 'em easier to put in a washtub.

I stepped in and smooshed the concrete around with my feet. Stomped it around a little. Moved my feet back and forth, like I was stirring it up.

"Stop dancing and stand still," said NASA.

"I'm just gettin' comfy," I said. "I'm gonna be standin' here a while, alright?" They laughed again.

"You guys get outta here. Meet back at my place. I'll wait for the cement to set." Sarge tilted his head for 'em to head on out.

"Really, it's concrete, not cement," I said. "Got gravel and sand, stuff like that mixed in it."

"That make a difference to you?"

"Not really," I said. The other guys were back up on the blacktop, walking away. Just me and Sarge were down there, and a washtub fulla quick-setting concrete.

"So here's the deal," he said. "I'm supposed to stand here and wait for this stuff to get solid, then I'm supposed to leave you here and let the high tide do its work.

"But that's one hell of a way to die, and you're not a bad guy. Plus you're a cop, just doin' his job. So I'm gonna knock you out first, okay?"

"Mighty nice of ya," I said. "Maybe I'll say a prayer for you."

Next thing I knew, I was dreaming about a huge dog that kept licking my face. I woke up with a mouthful of water. I coughed it out, pulling myself up to my elbows.

I was laying on the sand, and the moon was up.

The waves were washing up along my body, and every so often one of them would wash over my face. It was cold water, but I don't have to tell you that. And me out there in wet clothes, and barefoot. A man could catch a cold like that.

So I got up and walked back over the dune.

First, before I done that, I left my socks by the tub, 'cause they were ruined. I washed my feet as best I could in the surf, but walking barefoot through all the dry stuff picked up a layer of sand. When I got to my shoes, I dusted my feet off best I could and stuck my feet in my shoes anyway. There was nothin' I could do about the pants. The concrete pretty much ruined 'em.

The white pickup was in a driveway on Prortrero or whatever the hell that road is. Pretty much a good guess who lived there. I got in the back yard, and I looked through the sliding door. Three guys in there, watchin' TV. Ball game, looked like.

I wasn't sure if they'd be able to see me, so I tried to stay back from the windows. I snapped pretty good pictures of all three, a couple shots of each one, and texted 'em to Cortes and Sanchez. I threw in Sanchez 'cause Cortes might be dirty too, all I knew.

Then I sent *These guys tried 2 drown me @ the beach.* I also sent them both the address, and then I slipped back into the shadows and waited for the fireworks.

The doorbell rang. I said to myself, that's real quick. But it wasn't Cortes. The Captain walked in, big as life.

Well, that made it just dandy. So I sent another picture to Cortes and Sanchez, then another text with the address again, and I said, *hurry they caught me.* Then I walked over and knocked on the sliding glass door.

They all looked at me through the glass, like I had two heads or something.

Sarge got over it the fastest. He was up and had his gun drawn mighty quick. He yelled a couple times and Humphrey opened the door, slowly, with one hand behind him.

"You fellows wouldn't have a towel and some dry socks, would you?" I asked, as I stepped inside. NASA also had his gun out by then and had me covered. If I started doin' kungfu, him and Sarge both woulda shot me full of holes like that cheese with all the holes in it.

But they didn't want to do that. You kill someone at the beach, that's one thing. You kill somebody at your house, you got to hide a lot of evidence. Blood in the carpet, that sort of thing.

Captain was red as hell, and twice as mad. He looked at me and said, "I thought you said he was dead."

"Last we saw him, he was in ankle-deep concrete," said Sarge.

"I suppose he had a jackhammer in his back pocket?"

"Don't blame them, Captain. They killed me real good. Pro'lem is, I'm too smart for 'em."

The Captain said a few words I can't repeat. Might be children readin' this. Sarge grinned and kinda shook his head a little. NASA, he looked like he was gonna blast off.

"Oh, you're wondering about the concrete," I said.

"Yeah," said Sarge. "Seeing as we left you with both feet in a bucket, on the beach, at low tide, yes, we want to know about it."

"It's prolly still there." I looked around the room. "By the way, I gotta put all four of you under arrest. And since I'm outta my jurisdiction, I gotta detain you until the sheriff or the Highway Patrol can send somebody to make it official.

"So, let's see, you all got the right to remain silent, and to have a lawyer if you want one. Anything you say is gonna get used in court. And if you can't afford a lawyer — well, you guys say this stuff as much as I do. You know your rights, right?"

"Yeah, we know 'em," said Humphrey. He's got a grin now, and he's shakin' his head real slow, like, *can you believe the big brass pair on this idiot?*

"I gotta hand it to you, Licowicz," said Sarge. "Now we've gotta do this whole drama and kill you again, and this time, we got the tide against us. So tell us exactly what we did wrong."

Where I was standing, it was right between the kitchen and the den, where they was watching the ball game. There was one a them wooden stools there, so I parked my butt on it.

"See," I said, "When I was young and used to work in concrete, there was a guy who got his butt chewed for having a five-pound bag of sugar in his truck. Kept it behind the seat.

"So I asked him later, I said, 'What's with the sugar?'

"He points to the mixer. It's one of them with the electric motor, and it's on a trailer to haul behind a pickup. He had it wired where it could be turning while we was driving. Then we could just scoop it out for the customer, and off we go.

"He says to me, he says, 'If we get stuck in traffic, and that stuff is setting up by the time we get to the job site, I dump in that sugar. Then we can scoop out the cement with a shovel. Otherwise, we use a jackhammer.'

"So that's what saved my ass on the beach. Two sugar-shakers, two pitchers of syrup, and all those little packets. All of it, in my socks. Prolly that concrete won't ever set up."

Sarge started laughing. "Didn't want to ruin your good shoes. You crafty bastard, you wanted to make sure the sugar in your socks got all through the concrete."

"You figured me out, Sarge."

"And when we made you get in the washtub, and you were dancing around, getting comfortable — that was to mix it all up," said Humphrey.

"Bingo. Face it, I'm hard to kill."

"We'll kill you right this time," said NASA.

"And you're still mighty stupid," said the Captain. "Instead of getting away, you walked right in here. Did you really think we were gonna handcuff ourselves and sit on the curb while you called it in?"

"Funny you should ask," I said, and right about then the front door rattled like it was gonna come off its hinges. "Help," I said, real loud. "In here!"

'Cause, see, that give them the right to bust in. They heard a plaintive cry. That would be me, complaining. The emergency exception, we call it. Extramint circumstances.

Cortes was leading the way, and with his little nine-millimeter in his hand, but the guys behind him, with body armor and AR-15 rifles, tipped the scales into his favor. The four didn't even complain as they were cuffed.

Once they were handcuffed, I pulled out my cell phone and played back the conversation we just had. I dint know you could do that till Chance did it. Hell's bells, it worked.

Sometimes you gotta quit when you're ahead, and this was one a those times. We dint get another murder for two weeks after that, and by then, I cashed in my pension and retired.

Captain went away for murdering me, or tryin', and he got twenty for that. Sarge and NASA, they both folded. Humphrey had all three on his payroll. Captain actually pulled the two sergeants into it. I went to see Sarge while he was in the county jail, waiting for trial. Just so he'd know there weren't no hard feelings, him trine a kill me and me getting' him busted.

NASA and the Captain, they can rot. I don't even wanna hear their names again.

Sanchez offered to come back to Homicide, but I told her to stay where she was. Cortes had it handled.

That company that lost its gizmo – the toaster – they musta cut their losses, 'cause they never bothered me again. Me, I think Humphrey was a loser's cannon, and they dint know what he was doin'. He got twenty for tryin' to kill me, another twenty for killing Glennis, and another twenty for Merlot. And twenty more for Jaime Rosales, but he said just Sarge did it. Jury dint buy it. I wouldn't a neither.

I wound up payin' to put Glennis away. Figured I owed her. Her sister dint even come up from Arizona, if she's even there.

Me, I got me a nice place in San Diego now where I can sit on my porch and watch the ships go in and out.

The laptop. Yeah, turns out the security key was on a sticker on the bottom. I don't care no more about him havin' more pictures of me dumping bodies, but it turns out that formula they wanted, with electric symbols and pitchers and all that, that was there too, in the computer.

I'm thinkin' I might find somebody understands it, and see if they wanna buy it.

"Speaking of tall tales," said Chance. "A magic little machine that gives you pictures of crime scenes. That's some science fiction there, emphasis on fiction."

"And pictures of crimes that haven't even happened yet," said Bentley. He finished shuffling and dealt five cards around.

Yorga shrugged. "This is what Licowicz told me," he said. "You can believe it or not. He mighta been lying." He threw down one card.

"Or bluffing," said Jones. "If we're out looking for a mysterious magic toaster, we're not gonna ask how a guy with as many disadvantages as Licowicz managed to close 18 out of his last 18 cases." He threw down two cards.

"You're thinking he really might've been dirty?" asked Chance, raising an eyebrow. He threw down three.

"I know that Cortes always changed the subject if old Licowicz was mentioned, like there was stuff he knew and couldn't talk about." He kept one card and dumped the rest of them.

"So you're really thinking Licowicz played us?" asked Yorga. "Nah, I knew the guy. He wasn't that bright."

"That's what I heard," said Bentley. "One of the uniforms said that if the man had stuck to things he knew how to do, he'd have stayed home and ate pudding."

Jones grinned. "I wouldn't be so sure."

"Well, I'm sure of this," said Chance. "With that recording — even on suspension, he was still a police officer, and he still would've needed a warrant."

"You already had one," said Yorga. "For the wire in the diner. That should've covered it."

"Also, that Miranda warning," said Chance. "Pretty sure I'd never have got that tape admitted."

"You really didn't need it," said Jones. "The washtub was down on the beach, the concrete they must've purchased somewhere, and you had the direct testimony of Earl himself. That should've made 'em plead out."

"Well, I can't talk about what really happened," said Chance. "Professional canons and all. But Earl, let's say that he was playing a little loose with the truth."

"As a police Lieutenant, I have to enter a *pro forma* objection," said Jones. "We never lie."

"Yeah, yeah," said Chance, with a grin. "I believe my part of that."

Part III:
The Thin Client

"I THINK EARL MIGHT'VE sold himself a little short on the IQ he claimed," said Jones. "He was slightly before my time, but that doesn't mean that I've never heard of him."

"So, you've got some light to shed on the ballad of Elton Earl? I've got to tell you, this is starting to get interesting," said Bentley. He placed the deck of cards in the middle of the table and got himself another beverage.

"By all means, do tell," said Yorga. "I'd love to know what became of old Earl."

"He retired, but that's never the end of the story, is it? Got himself a place in Mission Beach, I think.

"Well, as police officers, we hear a lot of stories from a lot of people. I got this one second-hand, from that one mechanic over at the Work Street yard.

"He lived in San Diego before he moved up here; ran a muffler shop on the National City Mile-o-cars. Anyway, a fellow that used to work on his computers told him this one, and he passed it on to me.

"At the time, assumed it was a tall tale from a city full of sea stories. But now that I consider the matter, I'm fairly sure we're all talking about the same fellows."

"Fellows? Not just Licowicz?" asked Chance.

"Nope, your Fermat fellow as well. Anyway, here's the story as it came to me."

They say that in California, you can never be too rich, too handsome, or too thin. Well, I'm not so sure. I had this one client...

Yeah, I know, you think all IT guys are rich and rolling in cash. Well, the fact is, I didn't start my own dot-com. I'm never gonna write billion-dollar software. I'm not that good at being nerdy. In the land of the blind, I'm the one-eyed man. Plus, there's the murder conviction, and even if you get acquitted in a new trial, that never goes away. Not completely, not in some minds. Anyway, this one thin client...

"My boss likes really odd stuff. Got anything about the size of a toaster?"

That was her opening line, and it had me scratching my head. You don't get many requests for a toaster in a computer shop.

She came into my shop on a Thursday. I remember that, because I was trying to write a new flyer for mail-out on Friday, in hopes of spamming offices with it on Monday. I send a lot of spam. So sue me.

She was good looking, and there was no danger she'd ever drown, but she was a little too thin. She might have weighed a century, but I'd have bet in the low-to-mid-nineties. For a tall woman, five-eight or so, that's a bit skinny. Still, she wore it well. And she would never get a speeding ticket.

She looked around at the display models – empty cases, mostly, because processors go out of style too quickly to keep any real stock in a little shop like mine.

Her eyes skimmed the cables on the wall, in their cellophane bags. She glanced at the glass display case that I use for a counter. Then she looked me in the eye and asked for a toaster.

I cleared my throat. "We, ah, don't sell appliances *per se*," I said. "Though some of these processors make enough heat to warm your coffee, maybe."

"Not exactly a toaster," she said. "More like a DVR. It would be a little bigger than a toaster, have a USB cable, and a small LCD display on the front. All the controls are through an internal HTML interface."

"Sounds cool," I said. "I do have a few DVRs, none exactly like that, but some decent stuff." There's a TV on the wall behind me, and a wireless transmitter lets me project from my laptop. I turned it on and brought up my main supplier's web site, on the DVR page.

"Hmmph," she said. "Okay, to be honest, I'm not exactly looking for a DVR, so much as one certain DVR."

"A particular brand?"

"No brand at all," she said. "It was a research project my boss was working on, and it went missing. We've been checking computer shops in case it turns up."

"I don't really buy much used stuff," I said. "But I do take trade-ins now and then. I've got a old Merlin 6 x 20 phone system in the back. Not much call for them with everyone going digital. And I've got an ancient Bernoulli Box, with 10 Meg cartridges."

"10 Meg? You mean 10 Megabyte?"

"Yeah, back in 1995 or so, 20 Megs was your BIOS limit anyway. So 10 Meg cartridges were the bomb."

"That was back when people said, 'the bomb,' too."

She had me there. "I guess I'm dating myself," I said. "But that means I only have to buy one movie ticket and half as much popcorn."

She smiled, either in amusement or in tolerance. I didn't really care which. I was still recovering from an ex-girlfriend who framed me for murder, so I was somewhat immune to her charms. Jail trumps romance.

"I might also be interested in a used laptop," she said. "For example, maybe somebody came in with one, said it got encrypted somehow, maybe they couldn't remember the passcode, and maybe they needed someone to crack it."

"Any decent encryption and they'd be out of luck," I said. "All the major players use UFP and a 65-kilobit key. Unbreakable."

"I didn't say that maybe you cracked this hypothetical laptop," she said, with a grin that was dangerously friendly. Nice green eyes, under curly dark hair. Hint of flirtatiousness. A hint of a setup. "I only said that maybe someone brought in something like that."

"I seriously doubt it," I said. "When would this have hypothetically happened?" Even if I had such a laptop, I wasn't gonna admit it. For all I knew, she had a badge somewhere in that form-fitting outfit. Receiving stolen property is a bad thing.

"More than a month ago, less than a year ago," she said. "And odds are that the guy who brought it in was a retired cop out of Salinas."

"I'll check my records," I replied. "If it was a year ago, I've slept since then. Where can I reach you if I find something?"

She slid a card across the table. One side of the card said KARI in all caps. On the other side, there was a phone number with a 520 Area code. That's all that was printed on the card. No business, no address, no other information.

"Tucson?" I asked.

"Yes," she said. She smiled and didn't elaborate.

"What do you do in Tucson?"

"Well, at the moment, nothing," she said. "I'm in San Diego. But you can reach me right there. If that laptop turns up. Or the DVR, either one." She turned, walked out the door, and then glanced back to see if I was watching her leave. Of course, I was – I was wondering what her game was, and how it affected me.

When she was gone, I took photos of the card, both sides, with my cell phone. Then I dropped it into the cash register drawer, in the empty large bill slot to the left of the twenties.

The fact is, while she was talking, I did remember a laptop that a guy brought in. It was encrypted, and I told him what I told her – if it was a decent algorithm, nobody could crack it.

I remembered him, and he didn't say anything about being a Salinas cop, or else I might have thrown him out of the shop. He was an older guy, not exactly an old man, but on his way there, and he had looked like he had a love-hate relationship with donuts.

Licowski, Lisowski, something like that. Polish name, anyway. Licowicz, that was it. Right, Licowicz. So she was after old Licowicz. Followed him out of Salinas. Tucson to Salinas to San Diego.

I probably should explain my persistant disdain for Salinas' finest. I have nothing against police, and nothing against Salinas. But … Well, maybe I mentioned an ex-girlfriend who framed me for murder.

She killed a guy, got me to help her hide the body, and when it all came down, she put my thumbprint on the murder weapon, in his blood, and handed it to the Police. Said I made her help me hide the body. Played the battered girlfriend card.

I spent three months in County Jail waiting for trial. In case you're wondering, pre-trial fees for a decent criminal attorney are about 10 grand. Lawyers' fees in the courtroom are by the hour, on top of that. And with him bleeding me dry, I still got 25 to life.

My lawyer did me one huge favor, which was that he called the judge on a procedural detail – that is, he made an objection that got overruled. That was a favor because a few months later, I managed to get a 50-grand attorney for an appeal based on that objection – Yes, 50-grand: that's what the best lawyer in Monterey County charges for criminal representation, by the way, plus hourly in court – and seven months later, I got a trial *de novo*.

I had to have my lawyer translate that for me, like all the rest of what I'm telling you. It means they start over from day one and try it all over again, every step of the way, just like it never happened before.

In the eighteen months since the first trial, a couple things happened to torpedo the DA's case: First, my ex-girlfriend couldn't testify because she had started dating one of the cops, and her testimony was tainted. And even if they wanted her, she had moved to Vermont and dropped off the grid. Second, the cop couldn't testify because his testimony was tainted. Third, the evidence that my ex and the cop brought to the first trial, such as the murder weapon and the bloody thumbprint, were fruit of a poisoned tree.

Long story short, I walked on the second trial. Acquitted; not vindicated. There's a difference between not-guilty and we-can't-prove-it-but-you-did-it.

Well, I had to sell my house to pay for lawyers, and my business went down the tubes while I was in jail. I took what little cash I could scrape up and moved to San Diego, where nobody knew my name.

Now you know why my opinion of the Salinas Police is somewhat… Well, tainted, let's say. So, I run a tiny computer shop and I'm trying to get contracts for server administration with a few local companies, like I had in Salinas. So far, no one's biting.

The only reason I can afford rent on my tiny shop is that I worked a deal with the landlord, to manage his servers for free. I have a small van that I can park in the back storeroom. I sleep on a sleeping bag and an air-mattress in the back of the van.

Kids, don't ever help your ex-girlfriend hide her lover's body. Let this be a lesson to us all.

I didn't call Licowicz. I closed the shop and went for lunch at a fast-food place. I ate slowly and watched the doors. I then made what would have looked like a pub crawl, hitting about seven or eight shady bars in the Rosecrans area. These were places mostly visited by sailors, and mostly dead in the middle of the day. I had a ginger ale in each place and watched the doors.

One girl on the stage in one bar got mad at me, because I was watching the doors and not paying attention to her. I tipped her three bucks and left.

Satisfied that I wasn't being followed, I took a bus up to Mission Beach and went for a quiet stroll along the surf. Still no obvious tail, so I walked straight into the Sandy Shores Condominium Complex and rode the lobby elevator to the third floor. Licowicz lived in the second condo from the back.

I rapped on his door, loud because he might be taking a nap. Then I knocked louder, because he might be passed out drunk on his kitchen floor. Then I pounded on the door with my fists because I was pissed off that I drove all the way to Mission Beach for nothing.

The door across the hall opened, and an old guy looked at me through coke-bottle glasses.

"You lookin' for Licowicz?"

A few different answers popped into my head, like, *No, I'm checking his door for termites,* or *No, I'm practicing a drum solo,* but I held them back.

"Yeah, is he in?"

"Moved," said the old guy. "Iowa, maybe, or Indiana. Illinois? One of those I states." He closed his door, as if that settled the matter.

Okay. Fool's errand. I might have made some money if he had the laptop, but stuff happens. So I went back to my shop and tried to make a better flyer.

Around three in the afternoon, a guy came into the shop and started looking at things. He was staring at the serial cables like he'd never seen one before. Come to think of it, that might be true. Everything's USB these days, or TCP/IP. Or Bluetooth.

"Anything I can help you find?" I asked, from behind the counter.

He glanced over his shoulder at me and then turned back to the cables. "No, just looking," he said.

I looked him over, because people usually come to my shop with something in mind. I don't get many window-shoppers, and there's not a lot of stuff to browse through. But he looked pretty harmless, aside from his fascination with cables.

The sweatshirt was out of place, though. San Diego weather, especially in the summer, a tee-shirt and jeans is appropriate most places. A sweatshirt – well, not unless it's really windy, or you have circulation problems. But what the heck, he's the one that's gotta wear it. So I went back to putting stamps on flyers.

Another guy walked in. This guy was making a show of looking casual. Button down shirt, unbuttoned at the collar. Slacks, but casual slacks. Leather belt, gold buckle. A shiny gold watch on his wrist, matching the gold ring on his pinkie.

The first guy nodded to him, and there was some kind of signal passed between them. The sweatshirt guy moved to the doorway, and the guy with the pinkie ring stepped up to the counter.

"What can I do for you?" I asked.

"I'm looking for a present for my daughter," he said. "She likes computer stuff. Unusual stuff, especially."

I was thinking, *I'll bet she likes DVRs that look like toasters, and laptops with unbreakable encryption.* But I kept a straight face and waited for him to say more.

The guy in the doorway coughed.

"You know," said Pinkie-ring, "I just realized that I'm late for something. I'll come by, maybe tomorrow."

Sweatshirt guy stepped away from the doorway, and Pinkie-ring started to go around him, but two guys in suits were coming in. They gave Pinkie-ring a mad-dog stare, and Pinkie-ring just grinned at them. When they were inside, Pinkie and Sweatshirt vanished.

The first one walked straight up to me. He had a tweed jacket with leather patches on the elbows.

"Fermat?" he asked. "Donald Fermat?"

"Depends," I said. "Are you serving warrants?"

"Not today," he said, with a smile that might have looked friendly to some people. "Just need to have a chat with you."

"Then I suppose I'm Fermat."

The other suit, with sleeves a bit too long for his arms, turned from surveying the store and looked at me. "Were you up in Mission Beach earlier today?"

"Sure," I said. No point in denying it. They must already know all about it.

"What were you doing up there?"

"Do I need a lawyer?"

"Depends what you were doing up there."

"You know, fellows," I said, "My prior encounters with law enforcement have been less than pleasant. So I need you to tell me, straight up, if you're looking at me for something."

"I understand," said Tweed. "If I got twenty to life for murder, I'd be a bit careful too."

"I got framed," I said. "And it was 25, and later a jury acquitted me."

"Which is why you're down here decorating our fair city," said Tweed. "And we just don't want you to repeat the same experience."

"You don't want me to get framed by an ex-girlfriend? That's mighty nice of you."

"No," said Sleeves, with a toothy grin. "We don't want you to get acquitted."

"What my partner means to say," added Tweed, "Is that there was an attractive woman in here earlier today. What did she want?"

"That's a funny question," I said. "Just a moment ago, I had two customers in here that left when they saw you coming. I don't know what they wanted either. And now I don't know what you want."

"Did you know a man named Licowicz?"

"Do I need a lawyer?"

"That," said Sleeves, nodding his head towards me, "Is a question that only you can answer."

"Well, in that case, let's suppose that I simply decline to answer."

"We would have to make some assumptions."

"Assume anything you like. Assume a mortgage, assume a position, assume a hypothetical. But feel free to do it elsewhere."

"What if we assume you're hiding something?"

"I assume you can do that from down at the station house, right?"

Tweed broke in. "Do you have something to hide, Mr. Fermat?"

"I'm out of Easter eggs, if that's what you mean. Software developers decided that they were kind of unprofessional."

"So you aren't hiding anything?"

"I can neither confirm nor deny. And that's more than I intend to say, especially without a lawyer." I pointed to the door and tilted my head.

They looked at each other. Then they turned and walked out.

So what exactly did I know about Licowicz? Well, he came from Salinas and he was a cop; found that out today. He used to live in Mission Beach, but it looks like he bailed.

And he has a toaster that isn't a toaster, and a laptop that's like Fort Knox. Aside from that, nothing to speak of. So I got back to stamping fliers.

Postal spam, email spam, and fliers glued on all the local telephone poles would net me maybe six, seven sales over the next three or four weeks. Of those, two or three would be worth talking about. Enough money for food and laundry, since my rent was free. That's about it. I have a very tight budget.

I wasn't getting fat. Not by any stretch.

I closed up the shop at six. Not much hope of any real business after that. I counted my nickels and I had enough for a beer at the bowling alley, so I walked down there. And guess who was sitting there watching the pins fall over.

So if you guessed that it was a skinny brunette, you're dead on. I ignored her and went over to the bar. She got up from the little table above the lanes and took the barstool next to me.

"I don't sell toasters," I said.

"Sure you don't," she said, softly. "And a man can make a lot of money by not selling toasters."

"Oh?" I asked, not from interest, but in the hopes she'd realize I didn't have it and go pester someone else.

"Yeah, maybe even seven, eight digits."

"I've got ten digits on my hands." In case you didn't get it, that was a joke. I meant fingers. Of course, you got that. Who wouldn't? But she didn't.

"Where in the ten digits? One, two?" she asked.

"On my hands. Two thumbs, eight fingers, that's all ten of my digits."

"2.8's a lot, but any offer you've got, we can double."

"Nobody wants my fingers."

"Somebody I know really wants that not-a-toaster. They want it very badly."

"I don't have it badly or well."

"You said you had ten digits in hand, for that thing."

"It was a joke. My fingers. Ten of them."

The penny finally dropped. "Oh. Right. I'm so very disappointed, Mr. Fermat. I thought we were negotiating."

"Actually, I'm trying to get a beer so I can watch the ball game and then walk home."

"I could buy you another one."

"I'll be walking later. One's my limit."

"What about a slice of pizza to go with it?"

I was hungry, but not that hungry. "I'm good," I said, as a glass appeared in front of me. I nodded to a man down at the end of the bar. "Now, Doug over there, he used to be an appliance salesman. And he's never seen a pepperoni he didn't like."

"I'm not actually in the market for a toaster."

"Right, just a not toaster."

"You have my card, right?"

"Yup."

"Good." She nodded curtly to the bartender and then disappeared.

Well, the game didn't go so well. The Padres got shellacked. Then there was a shouting match in the bar; someone was there with somebody he shouldn't have been with, and someone else wasn't happy about it.

So I walked home. And things just got worse.

There was somebody sitting against my door. Just sitting there in the alley, back against the door, shoulders hunched, head slumped forward. It took me a moment to place him – I hadn't seen him in a while. It was Licowicz.

I reached down to check him for a pulse, and he had one in his neck. Plus he was still warm. I was reaching for my cell phone to call an ambulance when he suddenly kicked his leg and raised his head.

"Huh?" he said.

"Hello," I said. I stood still, waiting for him to explain why he was sitting there. Instead, he just stumbled up to his feet.

"Mussadozed off," he said, rubbing his face and running his fingers through his hair.

"Guy at your apartment said you moved."

"Yeah, he tells everybody that. Must be thinkin' of the guy before me. He's a little dotty, you know?"

"So he told you I came by?"

"You went by?"

"If he didn't tell you, why are you here?"

"Seemed like a good idea at the time." He took a couple of unsteady steps. "Oh, yeah. Gonna ask ya."

"You were gonna ask me?"

"Hmpf? Oh, yeah. My email don't work."

"Seriously?"

"Yeah."

"You bring your laptop?"

"Oh." He looked around, staggered a couple steps, and looked around behind him. "Guess I forgot."

I took his arm. "Let me get you to a cab," I said. "Go home and sleep it off. Call me tomorrow; I'll come around and look at your email." I started to lead him around to the front of the store, so I could flag a cab, when I noticed the door. Without Licowicz collapsed against it, the back door of the shop had opened and was standing ajar.

I said a couple of words I learned from a sailor.

It took the police an inordinate amount of time to get there. I put Licowicz in a flowerbed and left him sitting there, leaning against a palm tree. From the snoring noises he made, he might've been cutting it down.

I took a quick look. The storeroom had been gone over. Most of the boxes were off the shelf, and cut open. My van had all the doors open, and most of my personal stuff was out on the concrete floor.

I didn't bother going through into the shop proper. Anything broken or stolen in there would be covered by insurance. Well, hopefully. I went back and sat next to Licowicz while I waited.

If there's ever a professional snoring circuit, I'll put my money on him for the grand champion. Just as I was about to stuff my socks into my ears, he hit a crescendo that would of made him best-in-show.

It led into a snort, a cough, and a state that might have passed for consciousness. He looked around, gave me a glassy gaze, and slumped back against the tree.

About then, the black and white pulled up. I went inside with the officers and pointed to things that weren't like that when I left. I poked around, while they watched, looking for things that were missing. I didn't see anything that definitely wasn't there.

My small stash of cash was in my wallet, which had been safely in my back pocket the entire time. Aside from that, and the meager stock on the shelves, I didn't have anything else of value. You can't cheat an honest man, or that's what they tell me. Well, you can't steal from a poor one, either.

I told them about Licowicz sitting against the door when I got there, and they wanted to talk to him. Unfortunately, he was gone. Or maybe that was fortunate, since I didn't have to listen to him snore.

They asked if I knew anyone who might have been behaving suspiciously. I shrugged and gave them Kari's business card. I also mentioned two of their detectives who had been around, asking odd questions. They didn't react to my descriptions, so I let it go. Maybe the right hand doesn't know the left.

The fingerprint guy at the door shook his head, and indicated that he hadn't had any luck with any of the other obvious places to try. Eventually, they folded their tents and left.

I didn't open the next day. Since that meant not turning on the lights in the shop, that also meant I might break even for the day. I went out the alley way, carefully locking the door behind me. Then I knocked on the next door down, the locksmith.

His name's John Sherman, and as a fellow tenant, he let me in the back way. There was another guy there also, a sensei from the Kendo studio on the other side of me. They were having coffee, and John nodded towards the coffeemaker. I shook my head.

I gave him a brief rundown of my issue, and he recommended a seven-pin interchangeable core system that, in his words, "could give grief to Bosnian lawyers." I had no idea what that meant, so I just nodded.

It would be a pretty big outlay, but if it kept me from getting my place trashed, it might be well worth the investment. I agreed to it, even though it meant living on ramen for the next couple of months. I gave him my key, nodded respectfully to the sensei, and left the way I had come in.

Since I knew Licowicz was still in town, I started thinking about the sorts of places he might hang out, and a place called Diana's Welsh Pub and Grill, out on India Street, came to mind. I don't know why, but as soon as I thought of it, I could immediately picture Licowicz occupying a barstool there.

No tourists, no sailors; it was off the beaten path for both of those. It wasn't a dive where people get thrown out the windows; that would distract Licowicz from his serious drinking. It was just a casual neighborhood bar, dark enough inside that you didn't notice the passage of time, but with enough light you could play darts or billiards if you were really so inclined.

I caught a trolley out that direction. You don't care what line and what station, so never mind that.

I should tell you about India Street, though. You can't follow it from end to end, at least not in a car. It's one-way in places, and not always the same way. It also consists of about fifteen segments, separated by ravines, neighborhoods, and other obstacles.

I didn't remember exactly where to find Diana's place, so I was about four segments in before I found the right place. It was just as I remembered it, and for the first time since Amanda framed me for killing her boyfriend, luck was on my side. Earl was holding down a barstool, sipping a pint of suds.

The barstool next to him was empty, so I slid in and held up a finger to the bartender. Earl looked over at me, nodded, and looked back at the ball game. The Padres were schooling the Indians, and only two innings to go.

"Hey, Earl," I said.

He looked at me.

"So what the hell happened out at my place last night? Did you see who broke in?"

He shrugged. "I got there, they was comin' out," he said. "Three guys in baklava."

It took me a second. "Balaclavas?"

"Yeah, you know, like a turtleneck, but without the sweater. You pull it up over your nose and nobody can see you."

"Were they wearing anything else?"

"No, just black. Even the babushkas." I had a sudden mental image of three old Russian ladies wearing body paint and balaclavas, robbing my store and eating Greek pastry. Fortunately, about then, the beer arrived.

"So, you see anything else about those guys, aside from…" I gestured at my face.

"Other than the baklava? They was kinda small, maybe scrappy-looking, but kind of scrawny." He gave me a quick assessment. "Good thing you wasn't there. They'd a taken out a nerdy guy like you in a heartbeat."

"Taller than me, or just tougher?"

"Shorter. But way tougher, yeah. Lucky for you, you never been somewhere you had to fight. Like military, or prison or something."

I drew down the beer a little before I answered. "I did one year of a twenty-five year rap at Soledad."

"The hell you did." He looked me over again. "They woulda made marmalade outta you."

"I got lucky."

"Chaplain's pet or something?"

"No, I won my first fight, and never had to fight after that."

"You gotta know kungfu or somethin.'"

"Just got lucky."

"I gotta hear this."

"I don't want to tell it."

"You started it, so you have to tell it."

I chugged another inch or so from the beer and regretted mentioning Soledad. But he was right, I couldn't leave it like that.

"Alright. There was a Samoan guy, name of Samo. Big guy. Huge. He had a whole gang, all Pacific Islanders. Third day that I was inside, I'm in the yard, and he comes up trying to make beef with me. That's what they told me later. I didn't even know what that meant."

"Means he wanted an excuse to fight you."

"Right. I know that now. So he's walking up, pushing me back, waiting for me to take a swing. Like I said, this is a big guy, like six-foot six maybe. Four hundred easy, carries it like it's a buck fifty. This guy's got biceps bigger than my legs.

"He's actually bending down a little to be at my level. Tryin' to hold my eyes while he's pushin' me back."

Licowicz turned on his barstool to be able to look me in the eye. "Go on," he challenged.

"I know that if I keep backing up, I'm going to reach the fence. So does he. All his gang are chanting behind him, 'Samo, Samo!' They know it too: When we get to the fence, and I can't retreat, I'm dead meat.

"So I figure I'll try to get one shot in, and maybe I'll discourage him. Maybe he's like a shark, and if I bop his nose, he'll back off."

"Yeah, that don't work with sharks, I hear. Just makes 'em mad." He took a long draw on his beer, staring me in the eye the whole time.

"Well, I go in with a right hook, and I put everything I've got into it. He pulls his chin back, so instead of hitting his nose, I connect just under his jaw, about a third of the way to his ear.

"It's like … imagine you put a steak on a brick, and then punched it. It's like that. It's meaty, but it's solid underneath, right?"

"Waste of a good steak, you ask me, but you go and cook however. Get back to the fight."

"Well, I'm bracing for his counter, right? And he lunges at me, so I jump back. Except he's not lunging. He falls flat on his face. It was like felling a tree."

"From you punching his neck?"

"Yeah. And his boys, one second they're all 'Samo, Samo!' and the next moment, they're silent. So I had an idea, and I strike a pose like Bruce Lee, from some kungfu film. I've got one hand out flat in front of me, and I just raise my four fingers a couple times, like, 'Who's next?'

"Nobody gets up, so I walk away. Turns out there was a guard that they asked to close his eyes for a few minutes when they were gonna tune me up. When the guard looks back over, and there's Samo, face down, he blows the whistle, we all go into lockdown, and they cart Samo away.

"The bruise must not have developed under his jaw until too late, because they called it a heart attack. And his boys didn't say anything, because they thought I took out their top guy with some secret kungfu trick. Word got around. I never had to fight again."

"Okay," he said, upending the beer mug. "I gotta know. What really happened?"

"Well, I talked to a doctor later. Seems there's this nerve under your jaw. Vagus nerve, like Las Vegas, but spelled differently. But if it triggers, it slows down your heart. And it can even stop it. Well, I got lucky: I caught that nerve just right, and it dropped Samo just like that."

"I doan believe a word a that." He turned back to the bar and signaled for another.

"You don't have to believe anything," I said. "You asked, I answered. All done, all through."

"So you said you done one year of a life term?"

"Twenty-five, that's about close enough to life. But yeah, about one year. Little over. Got a new trial."

"Lucky enough right there. Don't go putting guilty Lily on it, adding in stuff about you killin' somebody while you was inside."

"It was me or him."

"Just sayin'. Story was simpler, I might buy it."

"I'm not asking you for a dime."

"So why are you lookin' for me? Aside from wantin' to know about them guys at your shop?"

"You remember that toaster you brought into my shop that one time?"

He froze. "Maybe," he said, and all of a sudden he was sober and serious.

"Well, some folks stopped around the shop looking for it. A couple of hoods, a couple of cops, and a skinny woman named Kari."

"You tell 'em where to find me?"

"Nope. Not a word."

"Probably best if you forget about me bringing in that toaster." The look in his eye said that he knew a couple of punchs that Samo never thought of.

"I was thinking, if you still had it, or could get it, maybe you'd want to sell it. I got the idea that these guys would be up for giving out a reward. Dunno about you, but I could use the cash."

"Yeah. Here's the thing. I went out fishing, and that toaster fell overboard. It's somewhere off Catalina Island about now."

"You always take your toaster fishing?"

"You got a problem with that?"

"It's a free country," I said. "Too bad. The whole deal coulda been done through me, you wouldn't have to be involved, and I'd split the reward with you."

"If they got the toaster, they'd want me with it."

"Maybe I fished it out of the bay and dried it off. Or maybe I went looking for you, and found it in your old storage locker."

"Too bad none of that is true," he said. "Because the best for all of us is if we both forget all about me and that toaster." He signaled for another round, and pointed to both of us. "But I'll buy you one for Merlot."

"I'm not a wine drinker," I replied.

"Me neither. I'm buying beer to remember Merlot."

"Your money," I said.

We drank our beer, toasting a grape species for whatever reason, and then I walked back out into the sunlight. It was getting towards midday, and it was going to be a warm one. By the time I made it back to the trolley line, I'd walked off the alcohol, and I was feeling like something more in the way of food.

I splurged on a Doodleburger meal, and ate it while I rode downtown. The rest of the week would have to be ramen and rice, to get my budget back on track.

I got my new keys from the locksmith and let myself in. The place was kind of cool, after the long hot walk from the trolley station. I locked myself in, had a glass of tapwater, and sat down to do invoices. Next thing I knew, it was dark, and I was snoring.

There was an urgent tapping on the glass out front, so I walked out to see what was going on. Kari was out on the sidewalk in front of the shop tapping on the glass door with something metal.

I flicked on a light and walked through the store.

"We're closed," I said, through the glass.

"You've been closed all day," she said. "Come on, Don. I just want to talk."

"I don't want to talk, and I don't have a toaster."

"But you know who does." She paused, and then she grinned. She must have seen that her shot hit the mark. "Come on, Don, just for a minute. I promise to be nice."

Against my better judgement, I let her in.

"I don't have the toaster," I said, locking the door behind her. "You know that, because your guys have already been through my shop."

"That wasn't us," she said.

"I'm getting a little curious about who 'us' is, if I'm being honest with you, Kari."

"Kari? Oh, from the card. Right."

"Yes, I got your name off of the card you gave me, with your name on it."

"And you gave the card to the police."

"Well, you broke into my shop."

"I did – we did nothing of the sort."

"Again, who exactly is 'we?'"

138

"My employer and me."

"Your employer, who doesn't even blink at offering me 6 billion dollars for a toaster."

"I'm the one who didn't blink," she said. "But he wouldn't either. The main thing was to get you talking about money."

"There's no point in talking about money, because, and I feel like I've mentioned this before: I don't have your toaster."

"But you've seen him. That detective."

"What makes you think so?"

"When someone thinks you may have found their hidden secret, the first thing they do is to go check their hidden secret. And you were gone for a long time today."

"Did you have me followed?"

"No, of course not. I'm terrible at that sort of thing."

"So …"

"But that doesn't mean that *they* didn't. And any offer they make, we can match. Or better."

"I really feel like I've missed the first chapter of this drama. Is there a TL;DR?"

"Could we possibly sit down? I'm tired of standing."

I stepped into the back, and got her the chair I use at my desk. I sat down on the tall stool behind my glass counter. Since I was playing the proper host, I went back again and brought two glasses of tapwater.

"Sorry it's not beer or Merlot or something," I said.

She grinned. "Oh, it's really too bad it's not Merlot." She sipped the water. "I'd love to see him alive and well after all this time."

"Him? I meant the wine."

"Yes, but you've been talking to someone," she said, waggling her finger at me like I had been a naughty puppy. "You've been talking to that detective. The one who knew Merlot."

About then the penny dropped. Back at the bar, we weren't toasting the wine; we were remembering a lost friend. Suddenly it wasn't so weird.

"Someone might've mentioned the name."

"Now he was very a naughty boy, Old Chris Merlot. He was the chief engineer on a little project that we had going. And one day, he picks up the prototype and disappears. Can you imagine?"

"I guess," I said. Now that she caught me on the Merlot slip, I was being doubly careful not to give anything else away.

"And then there came a reckoning. I suppose that the detective told you about that?"

I shook my head. "I don't know anything."

"Well, anyway, Merlot's dead."

"I guessed that much."

"Really? How?" Her eyes twinkled, like she had set another trap for me.

"Never mind how. Go on with your story."

"They say that history repeats itself."

"I'm hoping that's not a threat."

"Nope. Merely a remark. It's kind of odd, the way things happened. But anyway, the detective was the last person seen with that toaster. There was a fire, and we assumed that the toaster was lost."

"We still just means you and your boss?"

"Correct. But the toaster phoned home, just a few months ago. And from right here in this little shop. Pretty weird, huh?"

"What does it do?"

"Oh, nothing important. Just computer things. Too technical for me."

"Unimportant little computer things that are worth six billion dollars to the right people."

"Well, no one really understands the technical parts, right?" She shrugged. "But we want it. And it was here. So, Don, that means that you're not telling me all that you know. And other people also know that it was here."

"Well, there are lots of things that have been here, and most of them aren't here anymore."

"Here's the thing, Don. We just want it back, and we're willing to be very nice to people who help with that. On the other hand, our competitors, they're not so friendly. They tend to take a more aggressive view of what belongs to other people."

"So you're saying that I can sell it to you, or have it stolen by them."

"That's pretty much it." She took another sip of the water. "You really should get a water filter."

"I'm lucky I can afford the water."

"That's really funny," she said. "Ever thought about doing standup?"

"Not recently, but if it pays better than this…"

"You know where the real money is: It's in giving me what I want. Buckets of cold, hard cash. For one little laptop. Or one little toaster."

"Look, Kari, I can't help you. I don't know where those things are. Obviously, they're not here, or your friends would've found 'em. I'm out of this."

"You know where Earl Licowicz is."

"Like I said: I'm out of this."

"Think about this: You know those nice houses in Mission Beach? For a million dollars you could buy one of them. For a billion dollars, you could buy all of them."

"Well, a thousand of them. But how many houses does a person need?"

"You could use at least one more than you have right now, Don. Just saying." She produced another card from somewhere, and held it out to me as she got up. "I hope I'll see you around."

I locked the door behind her and shut off the lights. I stood by the glass windows for a few minutes, to see which way she went.

Honestly, part of me suspected she'd pause next to a darkened doorway, so that Tweed or Sleeves could light her cigarette. It was starting to feel like I was in that kind of a film-noir movie. But she simply got into a car and drove away.

The next day I opened at ten, and I had barely gotten back to the counter when the guy with the pinkie ring walked in. His friend in the big sweatshirt was right behind him. Sweatshirt started to look at the serial cables again, but pinkie ring coughed and nodded at the door.

Sweatshirt walked over to the door and latched the thumb-turn bolt, then flipped my open sign to the closed side. He sauntered back over near his boss, but at an angle, where he'd have a good view. And, I supposed, a clear field of fire, if things got ugly.

"So, um, fellows," I said. "I don't have any money."

Pinkie grinned at the thought. "We're not here about money. We just wanted to talk to you."

"Whatever you're looking for, I don't have it."

"I figured as much," he said. "Way too much traffic through here for you to still have the gizmo." He pulled a paper out of his back pants pocket. It was folded into quarters. "I'd just like you to have a look at this picture and tell me what you see."

I was expecting a photo of the gizmo, and I was actually kind of glad to finally know what all the fuss was about. But that wasn't it. When I unfolded the paper, the photo made me a little dizzy.

It was black and white, but it had a really fantastic resolution. Lighting was spot on. Part of my brain started figuring that it had to be somewhere around 1/250 and f11 or higher. But that wasn't the weird part.

It showed me and Kari. She was laying on my floor, over what looked like a puddle of blood. I was kneeling next to her, holding a gun.

I must have gone pale, because Pinkie Ring asked if I wanted to maybe sit down. I slid the stool over and sat on it. It made no sense. It had to be a fake.

Except that it was taken here, in my shop. From the angle, the camera would have been on the wall, above the serial cables, about ceiling height. I looked up there, and there was no camera. Just sheetrock, where the ceiling met the wall. Not even a pinhole.

"What the hell?" I asked.

"My thoughts exactly."

"That's not me."

"That is you, Donald Fermat. That's absolutely you. And the lady there on the floor with a bullet hole is Magda Grovich."

"I didn't shoot anybody. I don't even have a gun."

"Of course not," said Sweatshirt. "You ditch a gun after you shoot somebody."

He shook his head like I was an idiot. Pinkie Ring turned towards him and narrowed his eyes. Sweatshirt blushed and took a step back.

"Now, I'm not saying that Magda Grovich on the floor with a bullet hole doesn't warm the cockles of my heart," he said, with a wry grin, "But a man like you can't be too careful who sees a thing like this."

"It's a fake."

"Not a fake," said Pinkie Ring.

"You can't have a real picture of something that didn't happen."

"Sure you can. They do it all the time, up north in Tinseltown, right?"

"Those are fakes."

"Potato, rutabaga."

"Are you trying to frame me for something?"

"No, no, not at all, Mr. Fermat. You've got that all covered, all by yourself. But in the event that you should find yourself in a jam of your own making, well, everyone needs friends, right?"

"How is a fake picture a jam of my own making?"

"Well, you know, if you didn't want to be in this picture, maybe you might not want to pal around with Magda Grovich." He produced another paper. It was a different weight, slightly thinner, like bargain copy paper. It had a color photo, also rather nicely lighted, and also of me and Magda.

This time, it was taken from outside, and with a pretty long lens, because it made the shop look very shallow. It was in color. The light was tungsten, kind of yellow, and Magda was handing me something. Her second business card, most likely.

It must have been from the previous night, when she came to see me after closing. I was standing behind the counter, and the chair from the back room was visible through the glass. That matched my recollection; I don't think I turned on the overhead fluorescents, so the lighting would've been a little yellow, just like the photo.

Obviously, someone had been outside, across the street, watching us. Taking photos, maybe even notes.

"She was in here," I said. "She's looking for what you're looking for. And I don't have it."

"Funny thing," he said, picking up the two photos. "When that first picture was taken, the gizmo was exactly twenty-two meters away."

"When that picture was composed on a computer, you mean?"

"Twenty-two meters, Don. Think about that." He looked towards the back door, into my shop. "Maybe you have no idea what's around you."

He produced a business card. Like the one Magda had given me, it had a phone number, but the area code was 770. There was no name anywhere on the card.

He pointed to a serial cable, and Sweatshirt took it down off the wall. Pinkie ring threw a century note onto the counter.

"I've been looking for one of those. Keep the change. And don't lose that number," he advised, as he backed towards my front door. Sweatshirt was already there, opening for him and taking a look around at the street outside. "Call me if you get into a jam."

I did a quick mental inventory. I had a guy who wanted to be my friend, who gave out business cards with no name on them. I had a woman who wanted to buy something from me that I didn't have, and who gave out business cards with someone else's name on them.

And I made a hundred dollar sale on a seven dollar cable. Not enough to make me rich, but it might keep the day from being a net loss.

And I had had a peek at a photo that could very well be my doom.

Then I got to thinking about twenty-two meters, and I did a little math. For us Philistines that are still on the imperial system, that's about seventy-one feet.

Going one way from my wall, that would be in the parking lot of a fast food place on the other side of the locksmith. Going the other way, that would be inside the paint store two doors down, past the martial arts studio. Out the back, it would be in someone's back yard, and out the front, it would be across the street, maybe on the far sidewalk.

Was it within twenty-two meters, or exactly twenty-two meters? I didn't think to ask. And it didn't matter, because it was a put up job. That photo couldn't exist because it didn't happen.

But if a scene like that did get staged, that photo could sink me. I remembered Soledad, and the hospitality in the big house up there. I wasn't anxious to see if things had improved since I left.

Mexico was a short trolley ride away, and if I'd had a little money to make myself comfortable down there, I might have made a run for it. As it was, I could maybe get a decent hotel room for a couple nights.

Alternatively, I could head north. A hundred bucks of gas would get me, probably, all the way to Sylmar, maybe even Camarillo. Where I could work under-the-table in a computer shop and slowly starve while I lived in my van.

Really, there was only one guy who could get me out of this jam. It was a drunk ex-cop who didn't want to talk to me about it. I really didn't want to talk to him either, but it wasn't like I had a lot of choices.

"Dunno about you fellows," said Chance, "But I'm switching to coffee."

"Cup for me, if you don't mind," said Yorga.

"I'm good," said Bentley.

"Same here," said Jones.

"I've got to tell you," said Yorga, "I'm having a little trouble imagining a world where Old Elton Earl is the man who knows how all the pieces fit together."

"I'm telling you, Licowicz was stupid like a fox. If he ever scored 92 on an IQ test, it was to mess with the school psychologist." Jones shrugged.

"From everything I've heard about him, I'm not buying this either," said Bentley. "But it's a good story, so by all means, keep going."

Chance returned with a plate of cookies and two cups of coffee. Bentley took a cookie while Yorga adjusted the chemistry of his coffee.

Chance picked up the abandoned deck of cards and slid them into the box, as he nodded to Jones. "You were saying?"

Diana's place, it turned out, was a regular spot for Earl. At least, that's where I found him the next day.

"I thought I told you to forget you know me," he said, as I slid onto the barstool next to him.

"I've got a small problem," I said. "A man walked into my shop and showed me a picture that didn't make any sense to me."

Licowicz froze and turned towards me. "What kind of picture?" he asked, after a very significant pause. Not, "What kinda pitcher?" like he normally would've said, but "What kind of picture?"

"Me, kneeling over a woman who had been shot."

"You shot a woman?"

"That's just it. What was on that picture, that's never happened. It was like someone faked it, but if they did, it's a really good fake."

"It ain't fake," breathed Licowicz. He stared down into his beer and started shaking his head.

"I didn't shoot any woman."

"Not yet," he said. He looked around the bar. Nobody was near us, but he pointed to a booth way over in a corner of the room. "Go sit over there. You havin' a beer?" He raised his hand for a beer.

I walked over to the booth, and a moment later he came over with two fresh beers. I sipped from mine while he stared around the room for a while.

"Okay, look," he said. "I used to have this informant, name of Merlot."

"Chris Merlot?"

"How you know that? Yeah, Chris." He took a drink from his beer. "Guy used ta gimme pitchers of my crime scenes, but from when the guy who dunnit was still right there, doin' the crime."

"Pictures he had no way of having."

"Exactly. One time, he gimme a pitcher of me doing something, only I ain't done it yet."

"The toaster thing had something to do with it."

"Turns out that way."

"And that's why everybody wants the toaster."

"Except it's one of them Murphy's paw things, you know, what you ask for ain't exactly what you get."

"The monkey's there at the worst possible moment."

"Merlot used to say Murphy was a optometrist."

"Well, clearly, he could see the future."

"Yeah, and I think that toaster was his crystal ball. Okay, look, there was this woman he was seein' and after all the smoke cleared, I done some math."

"Math, like arithmetic?" I was worried he might've done some meth.

"Yeah, I dint stutter. Anyway, I tossed her place real good, the cops was done with it by then and her sister dint bother comin' up from wherever. And guess what I found, pretty as your peas."

"A toaster."

"Yeah, only it ain't got no bread slots. And it looks like the one burned down Merlot's place, only when you look close, not exactly."

"The toaster burned down Merlot's place?"

"Yeah, dint I tell you 'bout that? No matter, we'll get back ta that. Anyway, I think that one was the decoy, and this one's the real gizmo."

"So they both came down to San Diego with you."

"Right. So I'm parked across the street from you, that time I brought it in, right? Maybe down a spot of two, but you get the pitcher."

"Okay, with you so far."

"Well I get back to the car, and I'm puttin' it in the trunk, it starts hummin' and beepin' before I can get the foil around it good."

"Foil? Like aluminum foil?"

"I was keepin' it wrapped up in tin foil, aluminum, whatever. And also inside a cheap soup pot, you know, keep it from talkin' to nobody. Well, it musta called somebody in Tucson before I got it wrapped."

"And sent them the picture of me and Kari – I mean, Magda. And it took them this long to narrow down what shop it was, and who I am."

"Or why Kari was there. I'm sure they were askin' her lotsa questions, why she was in the photo, you know."

"So what do I do about it?"

"Beats the hell outta me," said Earl, into his beer.

Sitting there, I had an idea.

Here's a little detail about computer shops: To the average person, they're like a typewriter store or a dog grooming business. You see 'em everywhere, and you pay no attention. You just walk by.

But to a computer person, you have to stop in and look around, just in case they've got something you might need. Or maybe you use 'em as a place to network, and as a means to trade skills.

No one person knows everything about computers. It's not like you see on TV, where the guy who knows how to program your VCR also knows the top secret password into the pentagon's mainframe. The fact is, everybody's a specialist.

One guy, maybe he knows SQL really well – that's a database language – and he can make reports with all kinds of nifty data for you. Another guy is a hardware person, and can link seventeen SSDs into a RAID 3 array on a Linux server that works like magic. Another guy speaks ADA – there's a dead language for you – and this girl over here speaks cp/m with a MSDOS 3.3 accent.

You get the picture. It's like they all have common ground, but each one has their one special areas. So when a new shop pops up, you want to drop by and see what that guy knows, and how he might be useful.

Well, I don't know that my little shop was all that useful. Most of the nerdy folks who dropped by didn't come back around. But some of them left business cards.

There was a guy, I think his name was Nathan. He referred to himself as "The Worm," which is a game strategy in Risk.

The Worm is the player who never takes any area permanently, and just keeps moving his armies around as opportunity allows. That would be a contrast to the Corner, who bottlenecks Indonesia and locks himself into an Oceanic safe while the rest of the players take each other out.

To make a long story short, Nathan seemed like he might be a man who could tell us a few things about the toaster, and he might even have some ways to keep it from phoning home.

When I got back to the shop, I went into the wilds under my cash drawer and found his card. It just had his name and a crude drawing of a worm on one side. On the other, it had a phone number.

The phone rang twice, then there was a click and the ring cadence changed, the way that European numbers ring. You know, that buzz, buzz, pause; buzz buzz pause kind of thing. Then it rang normally, like a North American phone. After seven or eight handoffs that I could tell, I finally got a recording.

It made those three beeps, like Dee-DEE-DEET!! to tell you that it was a wrong number, and the normal thing about checking your number and trying again. Then it gave a single beep, and was silent.

"Nathan," I said, in the silence. "This is Don Fermat over at El Cajon PC and Electronics. Please give me a call. I have a business proposition." Then I hung up.

I didn't leave a callback number. Honestly, I'm getting used to cell phones, where you never have to. I just plain forgot. But as I was reaching for the phone to call a second time, it rang.

"El Cajon Boulevard PC and Electronics," I said.

"No names," he said. "Be at Horton Plaza, by the fountain, at six PM." He hung up.

By now it was about two, so that gave me four hours. I messed around in the shop until almost five, then gave public transit a workout. I got to Horton Square around ten till. I sat down on the edge of the fountain.

Weird little fact about the fountain: From the plaque, you'd think that the guy's name was Alonzo F. Horton. Fact is, the bottom part of the E was just below the water line, so it tarnished and blended in. The founder of the downtown area was Alonzo E. Horton.

Just tellin' you that in case it comes up on Jeopardy.

I'd been there about fifteen minutes when a bum came over and sat next to me. Really closely, like we were good friends.

"Be quiet," he whispered. "I have to check you for bugs." I almost said that I was more likely to get them from him than vice versa, but I let it go.

He put an arm around me, patted my shoulder twice, and then put his arm down. "You're clean," he said. "Walk down to the Broadway pier and start feeding the seagulls."

A small paper bag of peanuts fell onto the ground between us. It had a garish label, red and white, with a gold foil star in one corner.

Suddenly he scooted away from me, turned and put his hands up, as if I had threatened him, and backed away. When he was ten or twelve paces off, he turned his back and shuffled aimlessly towards the street. To an outsider, he had tried to befriend me and get some money, I threatened him, he left me alone.

In reality, he had scanned me from RF frequencies, and gave me the recognition symbol for the next cut-out. I waited a few minutes, and then began a casual twelve-block stroll down to the pier.

I stood at the rail and tossed peanuts, in the shell, into the bay for a few minutes, then a voice spoke from behind me.

"Hey, Don," said Nathan. "Good to see you again. How do you like spicy foods?"

"Well," I replied, "I like to think that I'm a man for all seasons."

He pointed me to a nearby Mexican grill, and the middle salsa, of the three, was a sinus-opener. The other green one was hot enough, kind of a tomatillo flavor, and the red one was obviously the mix for tourists.

He waited until we ordered – Tacos asada for him, and burrito al pastor for me – before we got down to the real business.

"So, you called," he said.

"I have some business that needs discretion," I said.

"I don't hack governments," he replied.

"Nothing like that. I was given a device. It phones home from time to time. When it does, killers show up out here in San Diego."

"Why not give it back?"

"Not really sure whose it is," I said. "Plus, it's a really powerful device."

"How powerful?"

"You remember that movie about that ring that had to be destroyed in that one volcano?"

"It controls dark underworld forces?" He raised an eyebrow, and we were silent while a waitress brought our drinks. "The eyes of Sauron are upon you?"

"Not so underworld-ish. But secret weaponish."

"And giving it to the wrong people…"

"Would be more dangerous than using it myself."

"But you need it not to phone home."

"Exactly. I think that maybe as many as three or four people might have died over this thing. Or more."

"A real monkey's paw."

I almost corrected him to Murphy's paw, and then realized that I was starting to think like Licowicz. Scary thought. "So I thought you might have a means to render it somewhat … safe."

"Safer."

"Right, you get my drift. Keep it away from the bad guys, and nothing bad happens to me."

"What are you doing right now to keep it safe?"

"It's wrapped up in foil, inside of a stew pot, and it's unplugged."

"How's that working for you?"

"Could be better."

"Okay…" He thought for a few minutes, and used the time inhale four small tacos on fresh corn tortillas. I got pretty well into my burrito before he spoke.

"Alright, I got it," he said. "Sisters of the Cross Two-seed Reformed Baptists down in Barrio Logan. They're having a potluck tomorrow. You walk in with your stewpot, right on through the kitchen, and out the back. I'll meet you there."

"And then what?"

"And then I give it a look over and see what's cooking. So to speak."

That gave me all night and most of the next day to persuade Licowicz. It took some fast talking, but when it came right down to it, he was as curious as I was.

Sisters of the Cross Two-seed was a tiny building that was obviously a church because it couldn't rightly be anything else. It had a small white-stucco chapel building with a steep roof and a belfry. On the side of that was an obvious addition, in red brick, making the original chapel into a tee-shape. On the end of the chapel opposite the steeple, where the pulpit would once have been, a large flat building attached. This was clearly the fellowship hall.

I led Earl down the sidewalk along the side of the chapel – the head of the hammer, if you will – to a double-door that had been propped open. It featured a panic bar, to open it from the inside, but the brass bar was dainty and delicate, a memento from another age.

Earl and I and the stewpot walked through the fellowship hall, ignoring the gaze of various church members, and right out the kitchen door, into a white van, where Nathan was waiting.

He drove us through a maze of side streets into a warehouse in the industrial area–and almost all of Barrio Logan is an industrial area–where we unloaded the stewpot onto a convenient stack of wooden pallets.

Nathan pointed to a small wooden enclosure in the middle of the warehouse, like one of those wooden mini-barns that you see for sale in hardware store parking lots. The inside was lined with copper mesh. There was a small table and three chairs, in front of an array of rack-mounted devices.

We put the stewpot on the table, and Earl lifted out a big wad of foil. As he did, some of the electronic devices started to beep and splutter.

"Nice," said Nathan. "It's phoning home."

"Shut it off," said Earl, lowering it back into the stewpot.

"Don't worry, I'm catching the signal." He gestured to the copper mesh. "It's only talking to my very-well-isolated sandbox."

Earl cautiously pulled the foil ball back out of the stewpot and put it on the table.

"Looks like the foil dint do no good," he said.

"The stewpot was a good idea though," said Nathan. He turned his attention to the laptop on his table. "Looks like a Tucson number."

"Makes sense," I said.

"This doesn't. It just sent three SMS messages. Looks like image files."

"You doan wanna look at those." Earl was insistent.

"But the metadata would be good," I said.

Nathan grunted. "Um, polar coordinates, hmm. Got it. I'll jot 'em down and figure 'em out later. We'll need to know the pole."

"I might have a clue on that," I said.

"Oh, the box!" said Nathan. "Of course; what else could it use for a constant? It's mobile."

"Right," I said, disappointed that he got it so quick. It's really not as much fun to be the second smartest guy in the room.

"And the images were captured... Last week, a week from Tuesday, next month." He blinked. "The date and time on the device must be off."

"Must be," I said. "We can fix that later. First, can you save those files to USB for me?"

"Guys, I need to know what this is all about."

"The less you know, the better you'll sleep at night."

"Yeah," said Earl, "Takes me two, maybe three shots every night. More than the usual, I mean."

Nathan pulled the USB drive out of the slot. "I was serious, Don, when I told you that I wasn't gonna hack any government systems. How do I know if this is spy stuff? Or something worse?"

"You don't. But the kinds of things you're thinking of, people don't need a super-toaster to make 'em."

Nathan nodded. "Okay. So what happens next?"

"As soon as we know, we'll tell you," I replied.

He handed me the USB drive, and Earl lowered the foil ball back into the stewpot.

Later, back at the shop, I dug out an old laptop. It had the wifi disabled, and it was permanently in airplane mode. There was no danger that it would try to get onto the internet. Also, if those little image files carried some kind of passengers – viruses, worms, that sort of thing – there wasn't much that they could damage.

The photo editor opened them easily. The first one was dated last week. It showed a view of a baseball field, from the center field fence. There wasn't anyone in the stands, and nothing was happening on the field. I studied it for a moment, trying to figure out if it was Petco Park, maybe, but it wasn't. Whatever park it was, the team that played there was away, or else taking a day off.

The one dated a week from Tuesday, about nine days away: I had seen it before. I was kneeling next to Magda, and there was a puddle under her. Unlike the one Pinkie-ring had shown me, this photo was in color.

The puddle under Magda was a deep red, which ruled out chocolate syrup. I tried to guess if it was enough to be fatal, and I'm no doctor, but I didn't think so.

She was wearing a pale blue top and dark blue pants, kind of an athletic style, with two white stripes down the legs. I was wearing a yellow polo shirt and jeans. Since I don't own any polo shirts, that was quite a relief. All I had to do was to keep anyone from giving me a polo shirt in the next nine days.

The gun – I really don't know much about guns, but it wasn't the kind from cowboy movies. I guess they call those revolvers. It wasn't one of those. It had a long, boxy part along the top, and it was entirely black.

The one dated next month – that was another matter entirely. But before I could get a good look at it, the bell over the door tinkled.

I slipped the photos into a surfing magazine and went out front to see who was there. It was the two guys in the suits.

"I take the fifth."

"Rightly so. It's gonna be a holiday," said Sleeves.

Tweed glared at him, then turned back to me. "So you want to tell us about this woman, here?"

I looked at the photo he threw on the counter. It was Magda. She looked a little pale, like she might be low on blood. But it wasn't the photo I was afraid it would be. I shook my head to clear the mental image of me standing over her, with a gun. Hopefully, they did not have that photo, or my goose was cooked.

"She looks a bit anemic in that photo, I suppose, but otherwise…" I shrugged my shoulders.

"A bit anemic. Ha. Gotta love this guy," said Sleeves. "Bet they loved that sense of humor up at Soledad."

"I heard he was just slayin' 'em up there," replied Tweed. "I wonder if they ever figured out what happened to 'Samo' Tu'gamala. Bet this guy told him a joke, and Ol' Samo just keeled over."

"Did I mention I was taking the fifth?"

"Don't do that. Just don't. See, my partner, he thinks he's a comedian, and you go making jokes, he's gonna ask if that's a fifth of whiskey, fifth inning at the ball game, you know how it goes. Help me out here; don't get him started. Okay?"

"I have no comment about anything. You guys might as well leave now."

"See, that's funny, too. You really need to stop. My partner, once he gets started…"

"Not my problem."

Tweed chuckled. "Oh, the optimism."

"Is that a threat?"

They both chuckled. "So, about the woman."

"What woman?"

"The photo." He waved Magda in front of me again. "Go ahead and tell me that you don't know her, have never seen her before, and wouldn't notice her if she dropped dead right in front of you."

"What happens when I do?"

"Then I pull out this photo," he said, showing me a photo like the other one pinkie-ring showed me; the one from across the street, through the windows, at night. Magda and I were sitting at my counter, casually chatting.

"Well, there you go," I said.

"So where do we go, exactly?" asked Tweed, leaning forward. "Do we go on with the next question, say, who you think she is and how you know her?"

"She walked into the shop one day, out of the blue, and wanted to buy a toaster. Never seen her before that."

"You don't sell toasters."

"Thank you. That's what I told her."

"So why did you keep seeing her?"

"She didn't believe me."

"I can understand that," said Sleeves. "'Cause I don't believe a single word you're saying right now."

"That's your choice," I said. "All I know is what I read in the funny papers."

Tweed waved the photo in front of me. "This doesn't look at all like you're casually chatting about you not selling her a toaster."

"You're serving her a drink," said Sleeves, pointing to the glass that I was handing her.

"Water. She was thirsty."

"So you offered her water instead of a toaster."

I saw a chance to see how much they knew. Clearly, they didn't know about the toaster, so I took a shot in the dark. "Well, I didn't have any Merlot."

"She's more the Chablis type," said Sleeves. "Maybe a nice grey Zin on the weekends."

"So take me back to that night," said Tweed. "You're just sipping a nice little glass of water with her, and you're explaining that it's not wine. And she says…"

"She says that she's in the market for a nice toaster."

"And you're saying what?"

"I'm saying that I'm sorry, I don't have any toasters, not even a bun-warmer. It's a computer store."

"What about a bagel oven?"

"Nothing even close. I mean, you get an i7 over-clocked, you run a memory-intense application, and you'll maybe get a warm chassis, but it won't boil your water, much less toast your bread."

"So why does she think you sell toasters?"

"I'm not that kind of doctor."

"What kind of doctor are you?"

"No kind of doctor, and especially not that kind."

"And how do you break that to her?"

"I simply told her I couldn't help her, and she should try an appliance store."

"And she just up and left."

"Pretty much. Now, if you gentlemen will just follow her example and move on down the road…"

They gave each other a look, shrugged as if to say that whatever happened next would be my fault, and strolled out the door. When they were gone, I looked at the metadata from Nathan. The picture of the ball field. What if there was a setting on the gizmo, to make it take pictures at a certain distance? Earl wouldn't know how to change that. I wouldn't know how to change that without spending a lot of time on it. And nobody else had touched the toaster.

That meant it would probably be twenty-two meters from that ballpark when the photo was taken. If the gizmo wasn't in the ballpark when the photo was taken, then that narrowed down where it was.

I did an internet search, looked up pictures of ball parks and then checked satellite maps for likely spots. Morley Field, near Balboa Park, looked like a pretty good candidate. It resembled the photo in my hand, and there was a parking area about twenty-two meters behind the center field fence. It was a very plausible spot for Earl to have been when the thing tried to phone home.

Why did he have it out of the stewpot? Well, I'd have to bounce that one off of Earl.

So it was a safe guess that the third picture – the one that would happen next month – was also twenty-two meters from the device when it was taken.

The photo of me kneeling over Magda was taken a week from Tuesday, but the device saw it when Earl first brought it into the shop. That was maybe eight, ten weeks ago. Plus the event was one week in the future. So, say eleven weeks. The photo of the ballpark was taken about two weeks before Earl brought me the gizmo, most likely. I could check that with Earl.

If that was right, the one that would happen next month was taken about six weeks ago, give or take. I felt like that should mean something. But for the life of me, I didn't know what.

That's when I thought of the laptop. Obviously, the purpose of the laptop was to control the gizmo. Somehow, maybe Bluetooth or something, it was setting the distance in time and space from the gizmo. That would explain how Merlot was able to get Earl's crime scenes: He would go to the crime scene, or nearby, and then set the time for minus twelve hours, and poof: Photos of the crime taking place.

So the next step was to secure the laptop.

It was also apparent that I was being watched, or else Magda was being watched. Pinkie and Sleeves had both had photos of me and Magda chatting in my shop. It was also possible that she was working with one of them.

I got a couple of cardboard boxes from the shop. One of them had housed a few dozen SSD drives. Yeah, I know it's redundant to say "SSD Drive," but it's rude to use a bare initialism. So you grammar nuts can... Yeah, never mind. Anyway, I got the boxes.

I lined one of them with a plastic bag and then looked around until I found a couple of scrap power supplies. My hope, when I put them on the shelf, was that I could maybe repair them – fat chance – or swap them to someone who would.

Didn't happen, wasn't likely.

They went into the box, and once it was sealed up, I supposed that maybe the box weighed roughly as much as a toaster. Who was gonna look closely, anyway?

I locked up the shop and let myself out the back. In the alley, the locksmith and the guy from the kendo dojo were shooting paintballs at pieces of cardboard. They had propped them up against the dumpster, and were taking turns making modern art. They both looked sheepish, and stared at me till I made my way around the corner of the building.

The trolley was five minutes late, but it got me to C street, and I made my way down to Broadway. The interstate bus terminal was very well-marked, and no one following me could have lost me. Not if they were any good at it.

They still had lockers, which was a relief. Most bus terminals have taken them out. I slid the box into a locker, dropped in two dollars in quarters, and pulled out the key.

I put the key into another locker, carefully pressing it into the folds of sheet metal above the door. To a hasty peek, the locker looked empty. Then I bought the key for that locker, and stuck it into my pocket.

I wasn't fooling anyone, of course. If I was being followed, the tracker would have seen the entire game. They'd bypass the empty locker, and simply pick the one with the box. If I wasn't being tracked, the bus locker trick was pretty obvious, and they'd still get the box quick enough.

Tweed and Sleeves, say that they found a locker key. They'd know better than to go to that locker. They'd just get a warrant, then have an eager group of cadets search every locker in the terminal, using the manager's master key. Magda, she'd tell the manager a story about a lost key, and get him to open them so she could check for her lost purse. Oh, that's it – did she say purse? She meant box.

Pinkie Ring, him and his boys probably owned the manager, or else they could let themselves into the depot late at night, after the last bus. Few locks can stand up to a careful and concerted effort to open them. Every locker in the place would be open by the time the depot opened in the morning.

One way or another, someone was going to get my box of power supplies, and then say a few bad words.

The quarters for the lockers about exhausted my cash supply, so I wound up walking back up to North Park. The nice thing about San Diego is that it's a very walkable city. It's also very wide, which makes for some long walks.

It was dark by the time I got back to the store. I let myself in the back door, and then everything went black.

I woke up lying on the cold concrete floor. It was still dark, so I didn't immediately know which concrete floor. I stood up slowly, and then groped my way towards a wall. When I found a light switch and flicked it on, I was the warehouse part of in my store.

The back door was ajar. By instinct, I walked over and closed it. A quick inventory showed that most of my stuff was still there. All that seemed to be missing was the locker key from my pocket.

My wallet was intact, and the one box on a shelf that seemed to be disturbed turned out to contain twenty-eight dollars in cash. I tried to figure out if I had misplaced the money, had hidden it there, or had been compensated for my headache. Not that it really mattered.

My phone rang. I didn't recognize the number, so I sent it to voicemail. The phone rang again immediately. It was the same number, so I took it.

"El Cajon Computer and Electronics," I said.

"That Tucson number?" The male voice on the other end sounded vaguely familiar, but I wasn't placing it.

"Yeah?" I asked.

"It's a LLC, subchapter S, called Keegano Artificial Research Institute."

"K-A-R-I."

"Right." It finally clicked; I was talking to Nathan.

"Any idea who they are?"

"Very hush hush research. No details."

"Government?"

"Nope, just spooky." I could almost hear him shrug. "Figured you'd want to know." He hung up without another word.

KARI. That made me think of the business card; the one that Magda had left. The fact that she asked me to call

164

KARI suggested that she worked for them. Now, I just had to figure out the other teams.

I made another box, like the first one, except that I wrapped this one in craft paper and taped it up for mailing. I wrote a return address on it – not mine – and addressed it to a random house in Storm Lake, Iowa.

Whoever had knocked me on the head either already knew that I had the key, or found it and did the math. Whichever it was, they would be at the bus depot, or getting warrants, as the case might be. In a few minutes or a few hours, they would know that the package was a decoy, and come back to see me.

If anyone was still watching me right now, it would be the other teams. So decoy number two walked out the door of the back door of the shop, at one AM, and made its way to a local shipper.

It was one of those places where you can have a business address that signs for your packages, or that will ship your package for a major carrier. They were closed, of course, but they had a large metal night drop box on the sidewalk outside. Decoy number two went inside.

Of course it wasn't going to ship; I hadn't put a shipping label, or even written on my account number. But anyone watching me wouldn't know that. With any luck, in a day or two, I could sort out all the teams.

Okay, there's a problem with having been inside. You develop a sense that you don't owe anything to anyone. If you got sent up unfairly, like me, that goes double. It's not that you feel entitled – that other people owe you – though that can be part of it. It's more a feeling that what happens to other people is their problem.

That's why it took me this long after seeing a photo of Magda, bleeding on my floor, to realize that I needed to warn her about what was going to happen. Don't get any ideas: I wasn't going soft on her. I just kind of said to myself that if someone knew I was gonna get shot, I'd expect a bit of warning. Fair's fair.

I had given the business card to Tweed and Sleeves. That was when I still thought Magda was named Kari. But I had the SMS metadata, and it looked like the same number. It should work.

When I first moved in, I found a burner cell in a drawer of the bathroom. You know, one of those phones for a pay-by-the-month service. There was also an activation card with it. I never really thought I'd need it, but I never threw it away, either. You know how it is when something looks like it could be useful.

I walked a couple blocks down the boulevard, and then over a couple streets. It wasn't far enough to be good cover, but it would give me plausible deniability.

The message was short and sweet. *Magda extreme danger next Tuesday. Beware of bullets.*

Then I pulled out the SIM card and the battery. It wasn't impossible that I'd need to get in touch again, so I put all of the above into a plastic bag and duct taped it to the inside ceiling of a newspaper machine.

It meant giving up one of my new dollar bills to get a newspaper I didn't want, but sometimes you have to make sacrifices in life. I'd been asleep about half an hour when my van's alarm went off, filling the little warehouse with reflected noise. I snapped awake, threw off my sleeping bag, and then spotted Magda sitting in the driver's seat.

I threw the sleeping bag back over myself. She hit the button on the key fob and turned off the alarm.

"Lucky thing no one sleeps in the kendo studio," she said. "Might've woke 'em up."

"What are you doing here?"

"You called. I came. 'Nuff said."

"What? No, I ..." and about then, I realized that when you've been up all night running packages around, and have gotten knocked out, and have just woken up from half an hour's sleep, it's nearly impossible to make up a good story.

"You realized that I'm in danger of being shot. What is it? Was there a wise guy in here looking for me, with his bodyguard? Did he say that unless I give him the gizmo, he'll shoot me?"

"No. Sort-of. Not exactly. He said ... Well, hell, let me get dressed and I'll show you."

She obligingly got out of the van and wandered around the warehouse until I emerged, picture in hand. I showed her the color picture, the one with her in a blue track suit, and me in a yellow polo shirt.

"How far away was this?"

"According to Mr. Pinkie Ring, about twenty-two meters. And it might happen next Tuesday."

"Not tomorrow."

"No. A week from."

"Well," she said, with emphasis. "It was nice of you to warn me."

"Suppose you do me a favor in return. Who's the wise guy?"

She ignored the question, still staring at the photo. "Do you own a shirt like that?"

"No."

"I didn't think so. Do you own a gun like that?"

"I'm an ex-con."

"Acquitted."

"That doesn't mean that the California DOJ thinks I should own a firearm."

"What they think you own and what you own could be two different things."

"It's not. Otherwise, I might take to shooting people who break in."

"Now, now, Don, that's not nice. Besides, you seem to be trying not to shoot me, based on the photo and the phone call." She gave me a toothsome grin that she probably thought was seductive.

"How did you get in, anyway? The locksmith said this locks were nearly unpickable."

"Not impossible. I could probably get them in, say, forty minutes to an hour. That seventh pin is a bear. And it's fifty-fifty if I'd actually pick them open, or just to the cylinder release."

"Nice to know that I didn't waste my money. So how did you get in?"

"You know the paint store down at the end?"

"Yeah."

"They've got terrible locks."

"Nice to know. But that's them, not me."

"All these buildings tie together. In the attic of one is in the attic of them all. The only thing separating them is a firewall. Lightweight girls like me can glide across the rafters and the headers of the partition walls."

"You cut holes in the firewalls?"

"Apparently someone was up there before me, Don."

Okay, that would explain the guy that knocked me out when I walked in last evening. He must've gotten in through that same path, ahead of Magda.

"Well, now you know as much as I know. If you skip town now, you don't need to worry about getting shot in my shop next Tuesday."

"One small little problem. Tiny, really."

"What's that?"

"Where's the gizmo?"

"I still don't sell toasters."

"Right. But the wise guy didn't give you that photo."

"What makes you think that?"

"The copy he stole was in black and white."

There was a knock at the door. Honestly, it was maybe three or four in the morning, and someone's pounding on the glass door out front. Magda gave me a wink and stepped behind some shelving units.

I waited a few minutes, checked that my hair had a pillow thing going on, to look like I just woke up, and walked out to the front. Sleeves and Tweed were standing on the sidewalk.

I pointed to the sign that said "Closed." They shook their heads. I pointed to the clock. They shook their heads again. Tweed held up a cardboard box. It was the one from the bus locker. I marked them so I'd know them apart. Okay, so they followed me, because I hadn't shown anyone the key. One down.

I trudged over to the door and opened it. They took that as an invitation and entered.

"What can I do for you Gentlemen at this ungodly hour," I asked.

Tweed gave me the stink-eye. "You could start by explaining why you hid a couple pieces of electronic junk in a bus station."

"I can't really say that I hid it," I said. "You obviously found it pretty quickly. And when people do that with luggage, do you accuse them of hiding their luggage?"

"Nice little stunt with the second locker, by the way," said Sleeves. "Slowed us down a little, but we knew you'd have a reason for locking an empty locker."

They hadn't gotten a warrant. The penny dropped. "You're not cops."

"Cops?" Tweed smiled. "What made you think we were cops?"

"We didn't show you a badge or anything, did we?" asked Sleeves. "We can't help assumptions that happen inside your skull."

"True enough," I said. "So get out of my shop."

"You invited us in," said Sleeves. "Besides, you don't really want us to leave."

"Why not?"

"Because if we leave now, you won't have a chance to tell us what you know. And we don't want you to lose that opportunity."

"What do I know, that you want me to tell you?"

"Everything."

"Everything I know?"

"We'll sort out the important parts."

"Okay. Let's see. An aardvark is an African anteater. Abelard, Pierre, was a lecturing priest in medieval Europe best known for his highly inappropriate affair with his pupil, Heloise. Antimony is a silvery metal – "

"We've got a smart-aleck," said Sleeves.

"You knew that coming in. And now, you need to be going out."

If they'd made an issue of it, I probably couldn't throw them both out. But they didn't necessarily know that, and it was best if they didn't realize it. For all they knew, I might possess that gun that I was holding in the photo from Tuesday, next week.

One way or the other, they left. I locked the door behind them, while wondering if it would be better to put expanded metal screens across the firewalls in the attic, or to chip in with the other shopkeepers to get the paint store better locks.

Given the common threat, maybe the locksmith would cut us some slack and hook him up at wholesale. I suppose I could also just give Magda a key, which would stop her going through the attic.

But that wouldn't help with any of the other rats.

I walked back into the warehouse, and Magda was sitting at my desk, thumbing through my invoices.

"Honestly, if I bought a stolen toaster off of Licowicz, you think he would've given me an invoice? The man's barely literate."

"Don't sell him short," said Magda. "His last year in Salinas Homicide, he went 18 for 18 on solves. That takes a little more than just police work. It's unbelievable."

"Alright, and he had the toaster helping him. Good for him. Still, why are you looking at my invoices?"

"Because I can, Don. Because I can. Also, knowing how you spend your money helps me know where you might hide things of value. Call it a financial personality profile."

"Profile me later. I need some sleep. If I let you go out the back door can I trust you not to come back in through the attic?"

"Alright, this time," she sighed. "But I can't promise to swear it off for good."

I handed her a small cardboard box from off of the shelf. "Here," I said. "Take this with you. It'll save me the trouble of hiding it somewhere."

I let her out the back, and locked it behind her.

I had dreams about roof leaks. Well, not exactly roof leaks, but attic leaks. When I got up for breakfast, I decided to start saving up my pennies to reinforce the security in the attic.

The rest of the week passed uneventfully. Well, I got an electric bill that shocked me, but aside from that one detail, everything was pretty normal. I even made a couple of internet sales, and with a slightly inflated shipping charge, I had a bit of green in my pocket, but it quickly turned into the water bill, some computer parts, and a large box of unflavored ramen packets.

Sunday evening, after closing, I was debating whether to boil one of those packets with some ketchup and soy sauce, or whether to try and fish enough coins out of the fountain in the North Park Community Park to make a Sonic run. Ramen and inertia were in the lead, but I felt like I really needed to get out of the shop for a little while.

That's the problem with working where you live and living where you work; your horizons start to shrink. So I put on a coat, let myself out the front doors and locked the shop behind me.

I remember crossing Howard Avenue, and about then everything went dark.

I woke up in a warehouse, tied to a chair. There was a table in front of me. On the table was a box, and it said that it was once full of computer parts. It was the box I dropped off in the overnight shipping box, the box that should've wound up in their dumpster.

So it looks like Sleeves and Tweed weren't the only ones following me that night. I tried to reach for the little pocket knife I keep in my pants pocket, but it wasn't there, and even if it was, I couldn't reach it.

I probably sat there, staring at that box, for about an hour before Pinkie Ring came in. He saw that I was awake, and walked across the room to park his backside on the edge of the table, facing me.

"So, I have to say," he said, "My associate was not amused to open the box that you so thoughtfully tried to send us, only to discover that it was full of electronic junk." He shook his head regretfully.

"I didn't actually send it to you," I said.

"Well, you sure weren't sending it to Magda or to those other clowns," he said. "At least, I hope not. And I'll tell you why: That would break my heart. It would simply make me too sad for words.

"And being too sad for words, I'd have to let Johnny express himself, you know, without any words. If you get my meaning."

"Johnny would be your friend in the sweatshirt?"

"Now that you mention it, my associate — not friend, that implies a degree of familiarity, and familiarity breeds contempt — My associate does have a certain penchant for loose-fitting garments. The better to hide things he might be carrying, if you catch my drift…"

"Guns?"

"Well. Things. That he might, or might not, at some point in time, be carrying. But that's enough about my associate. Let me tell you, he will be disappointed to hear that you awakened and that he was not here."

"I'm sorry to disappoint him."

"Oh, you will be, Mr. Fermat, you will be. Can I call you Don?"

"You may as well."

"So, Don, here we are, whiling away a lovely Monday afternoon, waiting for Johnny, and I'm thinking — "

"It's Monday afternoon?"

"Yes. I think Johnny might have hit you a little hard. We were starting to worry. I told him to check for any medications while he was there, in case you needed to take something, you know."

"While he's where?"

"In your shop, of course. We borrowed your keys."

"Couldn't get into the paint store?"

"Would you believe that they put in a camera system and an alarm? I mean, honestly, who does that?"

"People who want to prevent break-ins, I guess."

"So rude. Or *quel gauche,* as my old French teacher would say." He pronounced it "Kwell Gowchee," and while I'm no expert on French, I'm pretty sure that's not how you say that.

"So, anyway," he continued, "I was hoping you might tell us a little bit about where you hid the toaster. Or where you hid Lieutenant Licowicz."

"To my knowledge, I have not hidden him anywhere. You can probably find him in some bar somewhere. Look for cheap beer and sports on the TV."

He waved his hand. "Least of our worries. More importantly, suppose you tell me where we can find a certain toaster."

"I'd try an appliance store, or one of those big-box retailers. I think there's one up the street from ... Wait, where are we?"

"Nowhere you need to worry about. But you see, that sort of smart-aleck attitude, that really upsets my friend Johnny." Pinkie Ring made a tsk-tsk noise.

"I thought he was an associate."

"Absence makes the heart grow fonder. Besides, compared to how I'm starting to feel about you, he's like a brother from another mother."

"Speaking of your respective mothers…"

"No, no, no, let me cut you off there, Mr. Fermat," he said, talking over me. "If this discussion should ever get personal, Johnny would be very, very angry. And when he gets angry, there is very little I can do to help you. I cannot be responsible for what might happen should Johnny lose his cool."

He paused because his phone was ringing, and he walked into another room to answer it. When he came back, he looked angry.

"I apologize for the inconvenience, Mr. Fermat, and for the rudeness of leaving you alone, but I will need to step out for a few hours. In the meantime, please make yourself uncomfortable."

In his absence, I discovered that if you move your weight the right way, and point your feet, you can walk a chair backwards. I also found that if you do that too fast, it gets out of sync and goes forwards instead.

After what seemed like an entire afternoon of rocking this chair around, I managed to get next to the wall of the warehouse and find a girder with a rough edge. Several more eternities of rubbing the ropes against the rough edge freed my right arm, and after that, things went fairly quickly. Well, by comparison.

It was dark when I finally squeezed through a small window. It was a tight fit, and I might not have gotten all of the glass from the window frame before trying to crawl through it. I had a few scrapes around my midsection.

I was near the water, which narrowed down places I could be. I wandered around a little bit, making my way through a maze of chain link fences and outbuildings. I finally got oriented when I recognized the big hotel tower on Harbor Drive. That, the location of the water, and the fact that I was surrounded by warehouses placed me among the docks south of Petco Park.

It took me another half an hour, or maybe longer, to find a hole in a fence and to squeeze through it, and then a bit longer to find my way across the railroad tracks and across Harbor Boulevard.

The chain link fence snagged on my shirt and tore it even worse than the window had. It was nothing but shreds. I just took it off, used it to pat the scratches from the window frame, and tossed it into a dumpster.

I was about three and a half miles from my shop, as the crow flies, and about five miles as the taxi drives. Well, as a taxi would drive in LA or in New York. Streets in San Diego aren't like streets in other big cities.

In Los Angeles, if you get onto a major street, like Hawthorne, you can drive – or, in my case, walk quickly – for about eleven miles, through multiple cities, and the name of the street never changes. West Pico Boulevard, that's like 16 miles long.

In San Diego, every half a mile, major streets change names, change directions, or stop for a canyon, a freeway, or a park. Name changes and changes of directions didn't bother me, but the obstructions were sending me significantly out of my way.

My stomach kept reminding me that I hadn't eaten in nearly twenty-four hours, and I was getting a few stares, jogging down the street without a shirt. It's San Diego, and the weather was warm, but I was feeling a bit self-conscious, even in the dark.

Between the lack of shirt, the scratches on my torso from the window and the fence, and a couple days' growth on my chin, I looked a bit sketchy. It made me look like the sort of people police stop, to see what they're up to. Unfortunately, without my keys or my wallet, it would be a bit tough to explain what I was up to, so I really did not want that kind of attention.

I was keeping my eyes on things around me – for example, whether the car coming up behind me was a police car – so I completely overlooked the orange cones around the missing bit of sidewalk.

Faster than you can say words you shouldn't say around children, I was swimming in a mudhole. Barked my shins on the water pipes that were down there. They didn't seem to be bleeding, but my khaki slacks were now covered in mud.

The sides of the pit were slick and slimy, which made it tough to get out, but I eventually made it. I laid on the sidewalk for a while, catching my breath, then crawled up to my knees and stood up.

In the street light overhead, the muddy prints told a story, and I was pretty sure the utility workers would have a nice laugh when they got back the next day. Well, there was nothing I could do about that.

Now, in addition to being shirtless and scratched up, I was also muddy and my pants were soaked. I found a water faucet on the loading dock of a nearby grocery store. Nobody was around, so I managed to rinse off the mud from my face, hands, and head. I dabbed at my chest and tried rinsing the pants, but that wasn't so easy while I was wearing them.

There was a thrift store in Logan Heights. Maybe they would take pity on a guy with no shirt and muddy pants. Or I could offer to pay them Thursday for a change of clothes today.

They were closed, and I didn't have any money on me anyway, but someone had left a cardboard box next to the front door. It was obviously an attempted after-hours donation, the sort that thrift stores hate.

A sign above the box read, "Do not leave items when the store is closed." Somebody was hard of reading, or just didn't care. Normally, I'd have thought that was rude, but it was kind of a godsend.

I took a quick look, and found a shirt. Unfortunately, it was a polo shirt, but it was dark green, so it was no problem. As long as it wasn't yellow, I didn't need to worry about it being the one from the photo. Besides, I was planning to ditch it before I got to the shop. And anyway, tonight was Monday Night, not Tuesday.

I put it on, and while it might not have improved my overall look, it at least made me feel better about it. Or slightly better.

There was a pair of jeans that didn't squeeze me in two, and wouldn't fall down if I had to run. The legs were a little short, but I wasn't planning for a fashion parade. Now, to get home. Where, hopefully, I could get in.

My shop – home – was where my keys and my wallet were last headed. Or at least, that's where the guys were going who had taken them. Maybe I could get lucky, take one of them down, or get the cops into the store, anything to stop the madness and get my life back on track. Yeah, fat chance, right?

I stopped for a traffic light at Market Street. A pair of men dressed in pastel clothes came out of the laundromat and seemed to be staring at me.

"Hey, Noah," shouted one of them. "When's the rain gonna start?" The other guy giggled. I ignored them and kept waiting for the light to change. They had nothing better to do than to stare at a guy in high water pants?

"Color changing fabrics so went out in the nineties," he shouted. "It's like so last millennium!"

I showed them the number of friends they had before their dog died, then I jogged across Market with the light. But when I looked down, I suddenly got it. The polo shirt had a temperature-sensitive dye, and my dark-green shirt was quickly turning bright yellow from the heat of my exertion.

Well, some things you just can't help. And, anyway, it was Monday Night, so if I got home and threw this polo away, I would still be safe.

The street I was on dumped me into a residential area, and it took me a while to thread the maze. One of the blocks looped around, and I found myself going in a circle a couple of times.

There was one place where a major freeway cut through the neighborhood, and there wasn't a pedestrian crossing anywhere nearby. That one took me miles out of the way, and it's not impossible that I got turned around a little bit. My sense of direction has its limits.

Long story short, it seemed like forever and a day when I finally found myself on El Cajon Boulevard.

I slowed down to a walk, still several blocks from my shop. As I got to the shop, I could see that all the lights were on. Pinkie Ring and his maybe-friend Sweatshirt obviously didn't care about my electric bill.

My keys were hanging in the lock on the front door of my shop. I didn't see anyone inside, so I pulled them out of the cylinder, let myself in, and closed the door behind me.

When I turned back around, I spotted Magda lying on the floor, wearing a track suit like the one in the photo. There was a pool of blood under her, and a pistol – the kind with that sliding thing on top – lying next to her. I ran to her, checked that she was still breathing. For some reason, I also picked up the pistol.

Then it clicked. Me, in a yellow polo shirt, kneeling next to a freshly-shot Magda. I looked at the clock. It was 1:15 AM, Tuesday Morning. Crap.

I duck-walked behind the counter – I'm not sure why; it just seemed like what needed to happen. I called 911 from the landline, and put the phone off-hook. That should get a patrol car, and they'd call an ambulance. In the meantime, I needed to see what was going on in the back. My wallet was on the floor behind the counter, so I scooped it up and put it into my pocket.

I unlocked the front door for the ambulance, and carefully made my way to the back, gun held by my shoulder, the way they do it on TV.

From the doorway into the back, I could see that things were bad. Not that a lady bleeding on the floor in the showroom wasn't bad, but it got worse. The roll-up door to the alley was open, and my van was gone.

So much for just going home.

I stuck my head around the corner, and then quickly pulled it back. Boxes were opened, contents dumped out, and the warehouse generally raided. Even some of my ramen packets were cut open, and that made no sense at all. You can't hide a laptop in a packet of ramen. Or a toaster. Ruining my ramen, that was just mean.

Someone on my left shouted, "Hey!" just as someone on my right fired a gun. The shout made me duck. I poked my upper body around the doorway to the right, just as another shot dug into the door frame, about where my head would've been if I was standing. There were two or three other shots, with sounds of things getting knocked around in the warehouse.

I don't know anything about shooting guns, but I pointed it towards the flash from that first shot, extended my arms, and squeezed the trigger, all in one motion. It was an automatic, instinctive kind of thing, like I was trying to push the bullet at him.

There was a noise, like a groan. Things fell over and clattered around. I ducked back from the door and listened. It was quiet in both directions. I stuck my head around the corner and peeked right, then left. Each way, there was someone lying on the cement.

The guy on the left, once I got up the nerve to look more closely, was the one I called Sleeves. The guy on the right was Tweed. They were both in a better place. Or a worse one, depending. Probably the latter.

I put the gun I had in Sleeves' hand and pulled the trigger a couple of times. Then I went out the back, the way my van had gone. There were sirens up the block, and when they got to the store, I wanted the obvious narrative to be that three people broke in, and one shot the other two, as he was getting shot, himself.

Magda goes to the hospital, then to jail; the other two go to the morgue. All done, neat and clean, as far as the police knew. So long as nobody saw the fourth guy, which would be me, that was the story they've read.

There's a 24-hour taco place on El Cajon Blvd., called, I kid you not, Tacos-R-Us. It's next to a VW car-repair place called Bugs-R-Us. Real imaginative when they name stuff around here. I guess I should call my shop something like "Computers-R-Us."

Since I had my wallet back, I went into the taco place and ordered two carne asada tacos, with some pico-de-gallo on the side. It was only a couple of bucks.

It seems like a mighty blasé thing to do with the shop wide open and people bleeding all over my floors, but I was hungry, for one, and for two, this gave me a reasonable explanation for where I was when my place got broken into. It was only a matter of time before the police called and let me know about the break-in.

Since I lived in the shop, where was I when all this happened? Well, I stepped out for late dinner. Missed all the excitement and everything. Sorry, officers, I was here, having a couple tacos.

Plus, they had a bathroom, if you can call it that, where I could wash my hands and arms in case I had to take a paraffin test later. The cops don't use real paraffin anymore; now it's all done with cotton swabs and mass spectrometers, but you know what I mean. I wanted to make sure I passed the gunshot residue tests.

Remember, I'm an alleged former felon, with no second amendment rights that the State of California will recognize. Also, one of the things I learned from my acquaintances inside was to always wash away the gunshot residue. In the stories they told, that was rule number one.

In the meantime, while I waited for carne asada and the police, that left one important question: Where were Pinkie-ring and Sweatshirt? Well, that led to other questions: Why did they steal my van? How did Magda get there? What were Tweed and Sleeves doing there? So I guess that led to several questions.

But until the police were satisfied about the break-in, all the rest was secondary. My cell phone rang just as I was finishing the last taco.

It was well after sun-up when the police finally left. Once the last uniform was out and the door was locked behind him, I got the burner cell phone that I had hidden in the newspaper machine down the street, and I tried to call Earl.

"Earl's phone," said Pinkie-ring.

"Where's Earl?"

Silence for a second. "Earl's just a bit busy at the moment. Can I have him call you back? Assuming he's able, you understand."

"Where's my van?"

"A little ways out in the desert, off Interstate 8. If you turn left at the big rock, you can't miss it." He hung up.

The part about the big rock, I was thinking to myself how ironic it was for him to call me a smart-aleck. Along interstate 8, just about all the way between San Diego and

El Centro, there are thousands, if not millions, of rocks. Big ones, little ones, huge ones, enormous ones.

They are grouped in every combination known to man, and they stretch along the entire distance between the cities. They don't look like they should be there. If there was one of them, it would be a landmark. As it is… Well, anyway, all that told me that they were somewhere in the desert east of San Diego.

There was nothing I could do. Earl set this whole thing into motion, and it looked like it caught up with him in the end. I went into the back and rolled down the door. I wondered if one of the shelves might serve for a nap. Turns out, they work really well for that.

If I was lucky, I might get my van back, I supposed. If I could afford to get it out of police impound. And if there was enough left of it to make it worthwhile. Stolen cars that are recovered … well, you might not want them back, especially if they were involved in someone's last ride. For a moment I thought I'd have to go to Diana's place and drink to Merlot and Earl. Then I remembered something, and smiled.

Later that morning, I went to see Magda. To my surprise, she wasn't handcuffed to the bed rail, like you see in movies.

"Well, coming to visit me, that's sweet. But you should have brought flowers."

"Yeah, not really that concerned," I said. "More just kinda curious."

"But you did call an ambulance for me. That was very sweet of you."

"Well, the police did." I looked around, to make sure there wasn't a patient in an adjacent bed, or a nurse making rounds. "So what happened?"

"I went by and decided to try the door, since you got so testy about the attic," she said. "And it was open. With the keys hanging in the lock. You really shouldn't do that. It's not safe."

"I didn't."

"Well, I went in, hoping to buy a charging cable for my iPhone…"

"Wait, what?"

"That's what I told the police."

"Oh, got it. Innocent bystander."

"Yup. One of those guys in suits, he sticks his head through the door from the back, and shoots me."

"Ah. Then I come along and find you, the gizmo gets its picture, and I shoot the suits."

"Police seemed to think they shot each other."

"I might have staged it a little. Don't tell anyone."

"Your secret is safe. Where's Earl?"

"Earl, the laptop, the gizmo, my van, and the guy with the pinkie-ring, are all missing right now."

"Okay, look, Don," she said. "It's pretty clear that we're not gonna recover the gizmo itself. But if we knew for absolute certain that nobody else has it either, there's a nice reward for that, too. And let's face it, you could use some spare cash."

"Well, I gotta talk to Earl. Assuming he's still around. But I have a feeling that I can give you some assurances." I pulled a paper out of my back pocket and unfolded it. She took it from my hand gently, with curiosity, then bewilderment, and then a knowing smile.

"Earl made sure that nobody wins, didn't he?"

"Looks like it," I said. "Or he will, in three days."

The photo showed Earl on the back of one of those dinner-cruise ships that circles the harbor; dinner, dining, and dancing while viewing the city lights. Earl's on a back deck, below where the party's going on. His hands are wide, like he just dropped something, and there's a stewpot a few inches below his hands, like it's falling.

The image was taken about a dozen feet from Licowicz, and the metadata says it was taken at 12.41 feet from the device. Earl is looking right where the lens would be, if a camera took this picture. So odds are it was in the stewpot that he just dropped.

It looks like the device is somewhere on the bottom of the harbor, and it's a mighty big harbor. Seawater does horrible things to electronics, even if it could be found.

"Well, I guess that also tells you that Earl's okay," she said, with a smile. "I wish I could have gotten the device, but I guess this is good enough."

"It'll have to do. I mean, by the time you found that device, then all the work cleaning it up and drying it out, no guarantee that it works…"

"It would be easier to start from scratch, and this time, to make sure we don't hire a sneaky bastard like Merlot. I hear you."

"Sorry for your loss."

"These things happen," she said. "Just a part of doing business." She frowned. "What do you think happened to Pinkie-ring and Sweatshirt-guy?"

"I think Earl made sure that they won't bother us again. For a guy with all of his disadvantages, sometimes he finds an acorn." I glanced up at the clock on the wall. "Look, I gotta go. Need to open for business, if I'm gonna keep the lights on."

"Right. I'll be in touch."

I was in the shop, and open for business, for about two hours when there was a horn at the rollup door. I walked back and opened it up so Earl could drive my van back in. He put it pretty close to the original spot.

"Alright," he said, "Back to normal for now."

"I called your phone yesterday afternoon, and Pinkie-ring answered."

"Yeah, I was busy."

"Why did he have your phone?"

"Cause I said, 'It's for you,' and held it to his head. He was a bit tied up."

"I think I need to know more about those guys."

"Okay, well, they was a pair of goombahs out of New Jersey. You prolly figured that, from the wise guy stuff and the accent and all."

"I was leaning that way."

"Okay, well, they weren't connected, they just acted it. And I tole 'em, they didn't get outta my hair, some guys who really was connected was gonna hear about them pretendin.' See, the real wise guys, they don't like people puttin' stuff on their tab."

"You said you'd tell on them."

"Yeah. They had nothin' to do with this. They were sniffin' for crumbs. Everything they knew come from that Kari-Magda. Mustabeen somebody got onto it, they called Pinkie Ring, and it went on from there."

"Any chance they were working for her?"

"No, they stole some stuff that Merlot stole already, like papers. Enough to give 'em a hint. She had a file on Merlot, and they grabbed it outta her hotel.

"That's why they showed you a pitcher, only it was black and white. Merlot showed me a pitcher, it was always color. They just smelled money, and tried a deal themselves in."

"Got it. So what happened last night?"

"I come by yesterday? Monday, I come by Monday, you wasn't here."

"Yeah, Pinkie-ring was trying to sweat me."

"Well, I said to myself, I said, I'm gonna keep an eye to the ground and see what's shaken."

"Like a stake-out."

"Right. Well, that one goombah, he lets himself in with a key, just walks in, fancy as you please. I figure he's lookin' to do a once-over, only detailed. So I wait till he's settled in, and I go after him. He's sittin' at your desk, dumpin' your drawers on the ground and kicking things that fall out."

"That's just rude."

"Right? I mean, it ain't confessional." He shrugged. "So I put my off-duty against his head and ask if he'd like to go for a ride."

"In my van."

"Right. I dint have my car. Took the bus, you know how it is. I go all the way home for my car, what's he gonna do? Sit and wait, like a good little boy?"

"Probably not."

"Yeah, prolly not. So I cuff him to one of the back doors and make him call Pinkie. Then I break his phone."

"So that's where Pinkie-ring went."

"He came right here. Oh, right, he was with you. Yeah, so he comes in the door, bein' all sneaky like, and Sweatshirt's got tape over his mouth. But I get behind him, and next thing to know, he's cuffed like his buddy."

"Where'd you take 'em?"

"Out in the desert, few miles outside a town. By now they made it back to the interstate and flagged a ride."

"I hope so."

"If not, they can sit under one a them big rocks and wait. Plenty of shade."

"I was afraid you took them out there to, you know."

"Pop 'em? Who do you think I am?"

"Sorry, I dunno. My mistake."

He gave me a look like he was hurt; really badly hurt.

"Anyway, then I went where they said you was."

"Meanwhile I was running back here, and wound up saving Magda." I told him how things played out for me, but he was shaking his head.

"Look," he said, when I finished, "Like I tole you with your prison story, it's good enough, you savin' the girl that got shot, without guilty Lily. It ain't makin' the story better with you shootin' those guys."

"Okay, if I didn't shoot 'em, why are they gone? I'm gonna look mighty silly, telling you that they're dead, if they show up and start making trouble."

"Yeah, sure, you warned 'em off. Same as I did with Pinkie-ring and his pal."

"Who do you think they were? The suits, I mean."

"I'm thinkin' there ain't just one company doin' stuff like this toaster thing."

"They were the competition?"

"Yeah, and that's why they didn't even know as much as Pinkie-ring."

"Right. I mentioned Merlot in front of them, and they didn't even react."

"Prolly thought you was talkin' about wine." He glanced at his watch. "Speakin' of alcohol, you feel like a beer? On me."

That's probably all there is to say, except that about a week later, a package arrived, special delivery, signature required. It was from Tucson. When I opened it up, it was bundles of hundred-dollar bills.

So there really was a reward after all.

"You guys buy any part of that?" asked Bentley, looking around the room. "I mean, come on, guys. A magic toaster, for Pete's sake."

"Maybe, parts of it," said Jones.

"Yeah. Well, here's my two cents," said Bentley. "When I was seeing Amanda, one day she has me help clean out her storage locker. There's a TV in there, the old CRT kind. She makes me take it, and I've still got it, takin' up space in my living room.

"I'm thinking Merlot did that with something he stole, so that much is true: He stole some kind of high-tech, not a magic toaster, and got a girlfriend to keep it at her house to keep it on the down-low. I'll even believe he got killed over something like that."

"So, this TV Amanda left you, does it show you crime scenes? Like her killing her boyfriend and setting up her ex for it? Or burning down the Chess Club?" Yorga smirked and got up, reaching for his jacket.

"C'mon. You know what I'm saying. I'm just not buying that there's a magic toaster floating around out there somewhere," said Bentley.

"You don't have to buy any of it," said Jones.

"Yeah," said Yorga. "Maybe we're all bluffing."

-- 30 --